Fleur deKey

debuting amateur sleuth Echo LaBauve
and her
Insight Foresight Benevolent Foundation

vickie pettee

ISBN-10: 0989036707
ISBN-13: 978-0-9890367-0-2

Published by

Big Easy Press

This is a work of fiction. Names, characters and incidents are figments of the author's imagination. Locales are grounded in reality, flavored with artistic license.

♫♪

"Why fit in when you are born to stand out?
--Dr. Seuss

1

UPTOWN NEW ORLEANS: *after seventy-two years*

He flung the paper. His banging fist rattled the cup in its saucer, sloshing coffee over the brim."Damn. Now? After he's been dead for ten years?"

She stilled, tensed in anticipation. A quick sideways glance at her husband confirmed a fleshy face on the verge of eruption. Lips pouted, jaw clenched, he forced his breath out in snorts through flared nostrils. He deceived the community and his fellow politicians with his practiced charm while she suffered his mean-spirited nature in private.

After forty-three years of marriage, she'd learned to adapt to his deep prejudices and grudges by playing to his compulsive, self-opinionated personality. Maybe she could distract him. He usually settled down after the opportunity to espouse his grievance or sense of superiority. If nothing else, pacify his ego - long enough for him to remain calm until he left for the office.

"Another property dispute?" she asked as she buttered her croissant.

"Doesn't pertain to you, dear." he said with a condescending smile. His flared nostrils hinted at his suppressed anger.

The silence that followed unnerved her. Where was the explosion of temper she had learned to beware of? Her husband remained composed in his chair, refolding the newspaper neatly next to his breakfast plate.

She ignored his condescension, breathed deeply to calm her nerves and picked up the carafe to refill his coffee cup. "Just a reminder that today is my regular golf group and I'm staying at the club for dinner with the girls so I'll be home late."

He looked up as if surprised to find his wife still sitting there. With a dismissive flick of his hand, he instructed her, "See if the driver has arrived yet. I need to get an early start today."

Disbelief, rage and frustration skittered across his face, his mask of composure slipping once his wife left the dining room. Seventy-two years since the evidence disappeared. No blackmail or hint of a threat during his father's lifetime. Not even when Billy passed away. He had the derelict house searched thoroughly after Billy's death, relieved that old history had died with him. Where had the old musician hidden those items? Under a floorboard? In a wall panel?

The cigarette case in the newspaper article had belonged to his father. If the evidence was locked away somewhere by the key hidden inside the case, then he must regain possession of it.

♪♪

She waited until her husband was gone before she unfolded the newspaper to see what had rattled him. The human interest story showed a young man holding items discovered when his great-uncle's condemned house was demolished. Why did her husband care about this? She didn't remember him ever mentioning the Williams family or their property.

2

FRENCH QUARTER: *recognition*

"Good morning, Miss Margie," Echo called out to her neighbor.

She couldn't see anyone through all the foliage, but the water dripping from the balcony across the street signaled that her neighbor was watering her patio garden. White plumeria, creeping yellow jasmine and vining hot pink bougainvillea overflowed from the lower white wrought iron rails. A lush fern, small ceramic birdbath and bird feeder hung from the three arched iron lace cornices above. The patio lemon tree, pruned by Poppy into pom-poms, had recently been added to the right front corner of the mini oasis.

"Mornin'." Margie peeped out from an opening in one of the arches, pointing her arthritic finger up the street. "Somethin' goin' on at the Museum Store earlier."

Miss Margie's balcony view gave her an edge on the latest happenings in their neighborhood. Echo directed her gaze up Royal Street to the next block, but all seemed quiet. Few people were walking about. Too early yet for the tourists.

Stepping off her front stoop, she started the walk from the double shotgun house at the lower end of Royal Street to her Foundation office in the upper French Quarter. The aroma of stale beer mixed with soap steamed up from the sidewalk, a product of the awakening sun warming the freshly scrubbed concrete.

As Echo crossed Ursulines Avenue, her mesh Tevas sidestepped a puddle left by an early morning road sweeper. The weather report predicted high humidity today, so Echo wore her unruly ginger curls twisted off her neck into an oversize plastic clip. She dressed for street comfort. Walking or riding the trolley cars to move around downtown New Orleans offered more convenience than searching for parking space.

Today, a fabric purse she bought at an outdoor market in India during her and Hawke's honeymoon complemented her light cotton khaki pants and short-sleeve shirt. She admired the artistic combination of textures and colors and had delighted in bargaining with the vendor. The purse worn bandito style across her chest bounced against her hip. *I'm not exactly the model of sophisticated fashion preferred by Grandmother Esme.* She thought in defiance, *All I really need is something to hold my tablet computer, mobile phone, lip gloss and a scrunchie to manage this hair on humid days.*

She headed toward Sal's Market diagonally across the street. The small corner brick store is the demarcation point-- where the residential and business ends of Royal Street meet. Tourists rarely ventured beyond Sal's. They usually turned on Ursulines and wandered towards Bourbon or back to the French Market. Besides the physical boundary line, a natural time segregation occurred between tourists and locals. From noon to late afternoon, tourists line up at the short deli counter for Sal's famous muffaletta sandwich. The locals stopped in before and after the sightseers.

When she pushed open the door, the aromas and

product displays triggered memories of a summer spent in Italy. Her grandmother Esme had arranged for her to stay with friends in Venice as a 'finishing' experience after her senior year, but her favorite time had been the weeks spent at their farmhouse set in an olive grove in the small village of LaSterza. Sal's different sorts of salami, sharp full smell of Italian cheeses and the salty scent of the tiny purple black olives floating in brine in a barrel were reminiscent of a hole-in-the-wall shop in the Tuscan village.

Echo rounded the shelves stocked with Italian cooking oils and wines, plucked the *Times-Picayune* off the newsstand and headed to the back corner where a scrabble board and two racks of tiles sat on a stack of boxes. With the six letters selected from a rack, she played the word *simple*, and then flipped a chip to its red side. One rack is played only by short, balding, cigar chomping Salvatore Bertucci, the owner. It had become tradition for different customers to play the other stand of tiles throughout the day. A flat round chip kept track of whose turn it was to play – Sal or customer. Red and green, colors from the Italian flag, represented charity and hope.

Turning away from the scrabble game, to brag about the thirty-two points she scored for the customers' side, she realized neither Sal nor his wife, Bella, was behind the counter. Excited voices drew her attention to a partly open door connecting Sal's shop to the adjoining tenant. He normally kept that door locked.

Echo peeked through the doorway. A policeman closed his notebook and departed through the front entrance. She crossed the threshold into the Museum Store, careful to step around the items strewn on the floor. Someone had searched the cases in a hurry, she thought, observing the products jumbled haphazardly in the showcases.

The crown of her head ached like someone was tugging on a hank of her hair. A murky assault of her senses immediately followed the warning sign. A malignant undercurrent triggered her precognition of danger. Poppy called it her spacetime -in essence bending space and time where particles and matter orbit around her. Her intuition worked at warp speed while everything around her slowed down or hung motionless. Unable to control these unbidden transient moments which disrupted the fabric of her space and time, she respected and acted upon them. According to her grandfather, the white streak down the center back of Echo's dark ginger hair, is a blessing, not a curse. One of the traits she inherited from her Leger ancestors.

A short Italian woman hovered over a tall lanky young man with dark black skin and dreads, dabbing a cloth to his cheek. Archer Williams, the proprietor of Archer's Museum Store collected and sold Jazz artifacts-- some valuable to collectors while others were simply objects d'art.

In her soft husky voice Echo asked "Archer, are you hurt?"

"Not bad. I hit my face and scraped my hand."

"What happened?"

Sal and the young man spoke at once. Echo briefly touched Sal's wrist, quieting him. FLASH! *Rattled and worried.*

Sheepishly, Archer answered, "I came in early this morning to set up a Louis Armstrong memorabilia display for this weekend. When I arrived I found the glass broken and the front door swinging open. It didn't look like anyone was here, so I walked in. Someone must have been hiding at the side of the doorway. They shoved me down and ran away before I could get up."

"Don't you have an alarm?"

"Yeah," he said. "But only a silent notification to the monitoring company. Too many false alarms. The police said next one I'd be fined so I disabled the siren. The officer that just left discovered someone cut the telephone cable to the store, so the system didn't call the alarm company."

She twisted an escaped curl back into its clip on her head, taking in the disorder surrounding them. "Can the Foundation help?"

After inheriting full control of her trust fund three years ago at age 26, Victoria "Echo" LeBauve delighted her grandmother, a member of New Orleans' aristocracy, when she quit her job as an investigative reporter to create the Insight Foresight Benevolent Foundation, with a mission to *discover and utilize inventive and effective ways to help others help themselves.* Delight quickly morphed into mortification after Echo solved a high profile mystery and the locals adopted her and the Foundation as their 'go-to' for mysteries and puzzles.

Echo's version of a foundation didn't match her socialite grandmother's expectation. Grandmother Esme accused her of being an investigator without a license. *Well it did allow Echo to indulge her nine-year old dream of being like Nancy Drew.*

Grandmother Esme, owner of the Delahaye Academy of Etiquette and Protocol, had often instructed Victoria on proper social interactions. "A saucy, resourceful girl is welcomed. A snoopy, willful person can be offensive." Esme was very engaged in society. That's society with a capital "S".

Esme's father was a descendant of an old New Orleanian family. That scion came down from Virginia in 1803, when Thomas Jefferson sent her father's great-great-grandfather Jonathan Lewis to be a judge for the territory of Orleans after the Louisiana Purchase.

Archer wrinkled his eyebrows in puzzlement. He said, "I don't know, Echo. I can't make sense of this. Someone was obviously looking for something, but it doesn't appear they took anything valuable. What's weird is the only thing that's missing is that photograph I found this week when we demolished my great-uncle's old house."

Echo remembered reading the news article. Archer is the

great-nephew and only living descendant of Jazz Legend Billy Williams. Vacant, unattended and deteriorating for many years, the house had been the center of a dispute between the Historical Society and city government. The city finally deemed the property dangerous and ordered the house be demolished or renovated. The Historical Society wanted it preserved, but had no funds so Archer had no choice but to hire a demolition crew to tear the house down. The *Times-Picayune* had reported his discovery of a silver cigarette case in a pile of boards after the razing, publishing a photo of Archer with the case and its contents. Inside the case he had found a photograph clipped from a newspaper and a small key.

"Who was in the photo?" Echo asked Archer.

"Don't know." Archer shrugged his shoulders and said, "There weren't any names of the five people listed under the picture." He described the photo. "Three musicians posed on a pocket-size stage in a club - a piano player, guitarist and Uncle Billy with his trumpet. The other two people were a man seated at a table with a lady, who looked younger than all of them, standing near him. Oh, and the man at the table was the only white person in the photo."

Chomping on his unlit cigar, Sal chimed in, "He left the newspaper clipping on the counter when he closed up last night. Planned to show it to the old-timers who stop in here -- see if they could name anyone in the photograph besides Billy. Based on the clothes and bar scene, I'd say that picture was probably taken in the forties."

Echo asked, "Where are the cigarette case and key?"

From under the neck of his black t-shirt, Archer pulled out a brown cord dangling a small key. "Thought it'd make a cool amulet," he said. The cord passed through an intricate cutout design. The head of the key had been shaped into a fleur-de-lis. "The cigarette case is still in my car."

"What are the police doing?"

"What can they do," asked Archer "besides file a report about the break-in? Nothing of value was stolen." He looked shyly down at Echo, shrugging his shoulders, "I'm not sure there's a mystery here, Echo."

Echo's eyes crinkled at the corners, her full lips parted, revealing straight white teeth when she grinned. She didn't want to frighten Archer unnecessarily, but the malignant undercurrent she felt upon entering the store suggested something sinister was brewing. "Feels like a mystery to me." Reverting to her reporter habits, she rattled off several questions, "Why would someone want an old newspaper clipping? Were they looking for the other objects you found, too? Did you have any other items that belonged to your uncle which are missing?"

Archer walked over to a locked case, its glass top broken. Objects from the case appeared to have been searched and then dropped back haphazardly into the case. Archer lifted a drab brown wooden instrument case, beat up from decades of use, and brought it over to Echo for a closer look. "This belonged to Uncle Billy." A dull brass trumpet with a small dent in its bell lay on worn royal blue velvet inside the case. "Even after he became a more successful musician and bought another trumpet, he kept this case. My dad said he referred to his case as 'a friend I'll keep'." Shrugging, he said, "Seems odd. You'd think his trumpet would be more of a friend than his case."

The incident piqued Echo's interest, her intuition thrumming. She snapped photos of the trumpet, case and the disarray in the store with her smart phone, whispering "there's more to this story."

Animated by the mystery she perceived and troubled by the sinister fog she felt, she turned her earnest eyes to Archer, and said, "Let the Foundation dig around-- research to see if we can uncover any history related to the items you discovered."

When Archer nodded his consent, Echo pulled out her tablet computer, tapping her long slender fingers to open an investigative file. "Archer, I'd like to take the key and cigarette case with me, if that's ok with you."

Archer removed the cord from around his neck and placed the key on the counter. When he returned from his car, he laid the silver case next to the key. Discolored with black tarnish and corrosion due to long exposure in the heavy humid New Orleans air, the silver case measured five inches high by three inches wide. A lighter spot appeared in the center of the cover where someone had rubbed at the tarnish, probably in an attempt to read the engraved monogram. She snapped photos of each item.

Echo traced the monogram with her finger. The center letter *S* scrolled above and below the smaller letters *t* and *m*, on either side.

tSm

"Do you know who this cigarette case might have belonged to?" she asked Archer.

"Nah. I don't know anyone with those initials. Maybe one of the older musicians who stop in here might."

She jotted names of the old timers he listed to her file as potential people to interview. "It's Friday. Don't know how much I can find with the Satchmo Festival this weekend, so give the Foundation a few days to explore."

She picked up the key. FLASH! FLASH! Echo couldn't see auras like Poppy, but her brain often registered colors when she flashed. Brick red followed by peach – the colors of avarice and protectiveness.

♪♪

Turning into a shallow alley off Royal Street, Echo noticed that the wrought iron gates, set in a brick wall overgrown with ivy, were already open. The original stone fountain had been replaced with a lower profile one after Hurricane Katrina. Patches of algae had settled on the weathering grey concrete centerpiece of the brick cobblestone courtyard, slowly erasing the allusion that the substitute fountain was an imposter. Water flowing through a spout in the center of a concrete slab and over its edges into a wide deep bowl, created a soothing rhythm of sound. The three ceramic birds, added whimsy to the platform by the owner of a neighboring shop, often attracted other birds to the bath.

The Foundation office shared the cul-de-sac courtyard with two other brick buildings. Beyond the fountain at the far side of the courtyard, Corinne's Tea Muse sold teas and tea bath products from around the world. Round iron tables shaded by yellow striped umbrellas invited customers to sit for a tea reading by Corinne. The green window shutters of the Maskerader Shop on the left side of the gates were closed. Malcolm hadn't yet moved his costumed mannequins outside to greet visitors to his shop.

Her husband, Hawke, and Poppy had joined Echo in her search for an office for the Foundation. When they first visited this location, Echo immediately said, "Such a friendly space."

"Does have a welcoming ahhmmbiance, Shă," agreed Poppy in his Cajun speak.

In his quiet manner Hawke said, "Peculiar place for an office, but suits your quirky style. His photographic eye catalogued the possibilities of the space."

A scraping sound to the right of the fountain interrupted Echo's reverie. Zetta Hoang was standing a vintage 1960 Vespa Moped – repainted pink many years ago - back on its kickstand. She removed her simple nomad style helmet, shouldered her electric blue schoolboy leather satchel and headed to the office door. "Hi, Boss. I got your text message about a new mystery and already uploaded your file."

Maybe not the most flattering design for a short, slightly plump physique, the tie-dyed blouse and brief skirt over leggings were characteristic Zetta. She only shopped at vintage stores, saying "It's my contribution to the environment by recycling." Zetta wore everything she bought with a self-possession springing from perfect confidence in one's self.

Zetta placed her right hand on the security scanner unlocking the front door. Five feet two inches, spiked short dark hair crowned a round face. Wide set round brown eyes looked at Echo through today's eyeglass du jour, cornflower blue plastic frames. Zetta's mother had arrived as a child with the infamous Vietnamese Boat People, making Zetta the first generation of her family born in the States.

After convincing Echo to take Big Brush Charlie, a flamboyant French Quarter artist, as the Foundation's first mystery, Zetta then insinuated herself into the investigation. She proved to be an entrepreneurial researcher and tech savvy extraordinaire. Echo hired twenty-four year old Kimly "Zetta" Hoang and declared her CFO and Girl Genius of the Insight Foresight Benevolent Foundation. As Chief Financial Officer, Zetta managed the Foundation's investment portfolio and operational finances. In her Girl Genius role she maintained the high tech systems used by the Foundation and orchestrated background research for Echo.

Bip, Bip, Bip, Bip. Zetta punched in a code to deactivate the security system. They entered the office together,

The space with warm ochre plaster walls, painted concrete floors and the obvious absence of desks resembled a cozy great room more than an office. The only walls in the spacious room enclosed the bathroom with a shower at the left back corner. It had been Hawke's idea to convert the front display store window to a one-way mirror, allowing them to enjoy the courtyard view while blocking the intrusion of tourists ogling them at work. A bold mustard color leather couch, two chairs and a recliner encircled an irregular slab of polished cypress and faced an oversize, state-of-the-art touch screen wall panel comprising their 'work cubicle'.

Zetta plucked her remote keyboard from one of the eggplant suede chairs tapping a few keys, waking up the wall panel and displaying the investigative file in the monitor's main window. A sidebar showed weather, the Foundation's social connections and the ever present security system windows.

Turning right towards the compact kitchen tucked under a loft, Echo passed a short rise of wooden stairs with an open iron handrail that led to a shallow space upstairs which housed a network server, printer and other electronics that only Zetta understood.

As she rounded a counter height bar which divided the great room from the kitchen space she called to Zetta "Espresso or Café au lait?" She filled her own cup with hot water and selected an herbal lemon zing tea for herself.

"Espresso. Ok, I'm ready to hear about the mystery you stumbled upon," said Zetta. She settled into her favorite gaming recliner, expectant excitement lighting her face. When Zetta had added her gaming chair to the office furniture, Echo cringed at the boring black vinyl. Still navigating the boundaries of their relationship, hoping she wouldn't insult her new partner, she had asked Zetta if she could feel a disruption in their surroundings. The next week Zetta had the chair re-upholstered in an eggplant and celery green stripe chenille to blend with the couch and chairs.

Echo set the cups on the cypress table so she could remove the cigarette case and key from her cloth bag. She leaned back into the corner of the couch, sipped her tea and told Archer's story.

Zetta inspected the silver case, turning it over in her

fingers. "Did you have an 'IF' when you touched this?" IF - Zetta's acronym for *Intuitive Flash* – is how she described the intense intuitive insights Echo often experienced.

"Nothing distinguishable from that," Echo pointed to the cigarette case. "Just shadows. I sense contradicting forces from this key," she said, rubbing the delicate, scrolled design between her fingers.

"The person who broke into the store left an atmosphere that felt like muddy coffee. Oh, and Sal was worried about something this morning." She set the key back on the chunk of cypress and said "Let's outline our investigation."

Echo called out questions, her voice like a train with velvet wings. The list appeared on the wall panel as quickly as she spoke.

What special meaning did the cigarette case, key and photo have to Billy Williams?

Why did he hide them?

What relationship did the items have to each other?

Why does the key vibrate greed and protection at the same time?

What's so important to someone that they would ransack a store looking for them?

At the last question, Zetta interrupted Echo, "The usual motives. Money. Love. Fear."

Echo tucked her chin down to re-twist her escaping curls back into the clip. "Let's start by finding out who was in the photograph. Search the *Time-Picayune* archives for a replica."

"The T-P online archives don't go back that far." Zetta reminded Echo.

"Alright. You start searching online. See what you can find out about Billy Williams. I'll make the trek to the newspaper office." We'll regroup here later this afternoon."

The video telephony system chimed. His dark brown

hair tied back, Hawke gazed at them from the wall panel. With eyes the color of dark roasted coffee he searched the Foundation's space, softening when he found Echo. He looked over at her, his raised eyebrows mocking her and grinned. He had a thin upper lip and full bottom lip. His grin relieved the usual solemn, hooded look in his eyes.

"Going somewhere?" he asked when he saw her stuffing a granola bar and bottle of water into her bag. His long legs clad in faded jeans, a plain white t-shirt molded his lean taut upper body. Relaxed with a mug of coffee cradled in his hands, her handsome husband lounged against the kitchen counter in their cottage in Breaux Bridge. Hawke and Zetta had installed a virtual telepresence system in their homes, workshops and the Foundation office integrating it into their daily communications.

Echo recounted a brief summary of her morning and their mystery for the second time that day, gesturing with her hands to emphasize some points. Her face brightened, "I'm going to visit Mr. Earl in the T-P's archive cave. I bet he can help me find a duplicate of that old photo. Hopefully it will have a caption with names."

Her trademark streak and slanted piercing green eyes combined with the full lips of her wide mouth and slightly stubborn chin incited journalists to label her beauty as exotic.

Even though most of her friends and Poppy called her by her nickname, Hawke –like her grandmother- continued to think of her as Victoria. He had a vivid memory of nine year old Victoria's excitement when her grandfather nicknamed her for echoing his gravelly, off-key singing. Hawke had dared ask her, *Why do you insist on a nickname? Don't you like your own name?* She had declared, *Everybody in Breaux Bridge has a nickname except you, Mr. Smarty Pants.*

Breaux Bridge's telephone book is the only one in the United States that included the person's nickname as part of the listing. Hawke's mother, a full-blood Choctaw, thinking the small hook in his nose resembled a hawk's beak, had presciently christened him with a name that pre-empted the local culture of nicknaming.

Hawke certainly appreciated the willowy beauty of her body, he mused, but there was so much more to Victoria than her physical beauty. Her inquisitive mind and vivacious joy of life bewitched him when she was just nine years old. Her vibrant warm-hearted spirit now captivated his soul. But when on a mission, Victoria's absolute unwillingness to accept or endure any distraction, interference or obstruction, no matter who or what the source, crazed him.

"When are you and Poppy heading back to New Orleans?" she asked, breaking his reverie.

He said, with a patient smile. "When Rouge finishes his meeting with our caretaker."

Often Echo escaped to the cottage which Rouge Leger deeded to them as a wedding gift, retreating until Grandmother Esme's ire deflated from the latest situation. They were too busy to maintain the property themselves and at age seventy-two, Poppy needed help. They hired a caretaker and invited Poppy to New Orleans to supervise the renovation of their double shotgun house. Surprising them, he moved to the Quarter and embraced the rhythm and diversity of life in the Big Easy.

Hawke said, "My frames are already loaded and I told my parents goodbye last night."

A photographic artist, Hawke rented gallery space in the Lagniappe Marketplace, an old car dealership building in Breaux Bridge which had been transformed to spotlight small town heritage and local artists. Hawke's parents owned the property on the other side of Poppy's orange grove. Touted in a number of articles about the Acadiana area of Louisiana as being the finest in Cajun hospitality with diverse food specialties, their Bayou T Bed and Breakfast was growing in popularity. Salvaged slave cabins converted into bedroom suites featured many of the unique, original architectural elements such as cypress floors and 1949 newspaper wallpapering.

"I just wanted to let you know that when I get back to New Orleans, I'll go directly to the Horizon Gallery to help Elaine set up the display for tomorrow's show. Meet you at home around seven o'clock?" he asked.

She blew him a kiss, her eyes like dancing sunshine. "No good-bye. Miss you." The Telepresence chimed off.

Keeping to the shady side of the street, she headed towards Canal Street where taxis hung out. She walked the ten blocks, letting her mind wonder about the why and who of the break-in at Archer's Museum Store.

A construction area marked off with orange cones loomed ahead of her. She slowed her pace, oscillating between skirting around the construction to remain in the shade and crossing the street where it was safer to walk. An unknown infringed on her space, arousing her senses. She stopped and turned, searching behind her for what might have alerted her. Was someone in danger? Was someone trying to get her attention? Was someone following her?

This end of Royal Street was busier and noisier with traffic. Cars and trucks slowed at the construction site, but moved at a steady pace. A dirty white truck waited courteously at a corner for a couple to cross, then drove on. She detected no hesitation by pedestrians moving around her. Her senses cooled off and her spacetime smoothed out.

3

DOWNTOWN OFFICE: *tSm*

He growled; his face flushed with anger. "What the hell happened?"

The thin man stood at a distance across the office from the older, heavy man. He pulled nervously at his lower lip and said, "Archer arrived earlier than usual this morning. We couldn't find either of the objects you described in his store before he showed up."

Exasperated with the hoodlum who also served as his driver, the boss asked, "Did you discover *anything* at the store?"

Cautious of his boss' unpredictable reaction, he hesitated before speaking. "I hung around the Italian store after lunch. Seems Archer doesn't have a clue why his uncle hid those items. I overheard talk about a redhead who the locals believe has special powers. Hmphh. What superstitious baloney. Anyway, she has a Foundation, or something like that, which digs into mysteries. There was speculation that she took the case and key."

"So now we have a group of do-gooders interested?" The older man grimaced. He waved the cigar held between his thumb and forefinger, anger biting his words, and ordered, "We need to recover the key before fascination with those items grows."

"Yes sir." The thin man edged back out of the doorway, but the irate businessman wasn't finished with him.

"I did some research on the nephew. His business is barely making a profit. He had to borrow the funds to demolish Billy's house. My father was fond of saying *Money talks, bullshit walks*. Let's see if we can convince him to give up the items for cash before he becomes invested in the meaning of his uncle's action."

The thug puffed up his chest and hardened his eyes to express his self-assurance, "I'll take care of the bribe."

"Do it without identifying yourself. And don't underestimate that snoopy girl. She's like a dog with a bone when playing detective."

The stout boss plopped into his desk chair, the flush on his face slowly receding. He chewed on his cigar. Lips pursed in disgust, he contemplated the old newspaper photo sitting atop the monogrammed leather desk blotter.

Unsure whether he had been dismissed, the thug leaned his ectomorphic physique against the door frame and waited.

Finally, the man spoke around the cigar still clamped between his teeth. "Her Foundation has a loyal following with an incredulous belief in her ability to solve puzzles." He wagged his thick stubby finger in the air pontificating, "I don't believe that things happen because of luck, chance or fate. You be extra cautious." His voice and attitude hardened when he warned, "Do not cause anyone to look my way."

After his hired man left, he moved the photo from his desktop to a drawer, contemplating how he could keep tabs on the LaBauve woman. He wasn't admitting he believed the malarkey about her being an intuitive, but he resolved not to be alone with her. He figured if he surrounded himself with others, her senses might be confused.

4

ROYAL STREET: *disrupted harmony*

"March 1939 in the Lagniappe section of the news," a triumphant Echo danced through the front door waving paper then climbed the steps to the loft. A collage of photographs and very brief article appeared on the wall panel when she scanned them into an investigative file. Fanning her sticky shirt back and forth from her chest to cool her body, she descended the stairs and took a detour to the kitchen to grab a cold bottle of water before joining Zetta.

"It's a piece about Jazz musicians playing in clubs. They couldn't earn enough from their music so they worked other jobs to support themselves and their families."

Zooming in on one of the photographs in the collage with her remote, Echo told Zetta, "I sent this one to Archer's phone. He texted me back, confirming it's the same picture that he found in the cigarette case. Problem is there are no captions or names on any of these photos."

Zetta hopped out of her contoured recliner to interact with the large touch screen panel. "Orpheum Social Club, The

Open Door, Twenty-Five Club, Muskrat Lounge," using her finger as a stylus she underlined the Jazz Clubs mentioned in the article. With a wicked little giggle, "Bow-wow, a couple of these vintage club names should never be resurrected! I'll try tracing their histories. Maybe we can correlate one of them with the dudes in our photo or the monogram on the cancer stick case."

Sweeping the window on the computer display away with her hand, she expanded an obituary with a practiced movement of her fingers. In her sing-song voice, she said, "Billy Williams – no middle initial – born in 1917, died at the age of eighty-five in 2002." She calculated in her head quickly. "He's twenty-two years old in the photo."

She paced in front of the screen, ticking off other facts. "He played his trumpet across the U.S. and Europe, recording with some of the Jazz Greats and composing his own jazz and pop even though he couldn't read or write music. Never married, no children. Archer is the only living descendant and inherited Billy's property after his own father passed away."

Zetta swiped the obituary into a corner of the large screen, double tapping three articles to enlarge them. "These are different pieces about his house and the debate between the preservation societies and the City Council. It had been featured on a tour of 100 historic jazz homes until it was demolished three days ago. I'm not sure any of these are pertinent to our mystery, other than that the demolition led to Archer's discovery."

"But I did find this interesting." Zetta dragged a newspaper article with a photo of a much older Billy Williams to the front, tapping various words to highlight them. "Integrity. Compassion. Patriarchal. Champion. The writer focused on how much Billy's friends respected and admired him for his advocacy of fair treatment for musicians with the club owners and managers who were often shady or corrupt."

"You know," said Echo "that seemed to be the era. During our search of the archives, Mr. Earl pointed out headlines in 1939 and1940 about the Louisiana Scandals. A free-for-all period of corruption and graft. Hundreds of government officials and businessmen were implicated in wrongdoing, and some were indicted."

Zetta tagged the article with a yellow bookmark icon as a crumb of information to be further investigated. She perched on the chair and snatched her keyboard.

Dang-a-lang. Zetta often amused herself by programming comic sound affects in their various applications.

"Blast from the Past," she keyed into their status and posted the photograph clipping on the Foundation's facebook page. "Can you name any of these people?" With a popular following, many online 'friends' participated online in the Insight Foresight Foundation mysteries.

Uncurling her long legs from beneath her on the couch, Echo stretched her arms high above her head, twisting her head back and forth to release the kink in her neck. "Enough for today, I think." She asked Zetta, "Will you be at Hawke's show tomorrow night?"

Zetta placed her hand over her heart, exaggerated a long audible sigh, and teased, "Boss, even if his photography was awful, I'd go just to see that beautiful man hunk of yours."

Echo wagged her finger at Zetta, and with a chuckle quoted Dr Seuss, "Be who you are and say what you feel because those who mind don't matter and those who matter don't mind."

John and Bella Delahaye had encouraged Echo's natural inquisitiveness by introducing her to books, agreeing with Dr. Seuss, *The more that you read, the more things you will know. The more that you learn the more places you'll go.* Poppy said Victoria's penchant for quoting Dr. Seuss was her way of keeping alive memories of her parents.

Zetta flipped her hand in a childish manner shooing Echo out the door, muttering, "You don't have to get all Seussy on me."

♫♪

Victoria paused at the street corner; standing very still, closed her eyes, slowed her breathing and assessed all that her senses had experienced in the last fifteen minutes on her walk home. Instinct was nipping at her conscious thought.

Was someone following her? Slowly turning in a circle she scanned the sidewalks on both sides of the street, watching as people moved around her. Nothing appeared unusual. She walked the next half block and on impulse decided to stop and check in with Archer.

Echo stepped around the repairman replacing the glass on the front door. The aisle floors were cleared, broken glass swept away. "I'm on my way home and thought I'd see how you're doing." called Echo striding into his store. She paused, expecting a murky air to envelope her. Nothing.

Archer looked up from the counter where he was straightening the disarray, his cheek swollen with a small cut on his chin. Seeing her concerned expression, he reassured her, "My face will heal. Nothing serious. Took me a while to clean up the store, though."

"Did you discover anything else missing?" asked Echo.

"Nope."

"I thought you'd like another copy of the photo," she told Archer, handing Archer a printout of the newspaper clipping.

He took the picture, walked to the front of the store. Archer fiddled with an acrylic frame he pulled out from under the counter.

Something is off, Echo thought. He was avoiding her eyes

and touch. She said, "Let me know if one of your regulars recognizes any of the people or the location in the picture."

Archer finally looked up. He cleared his throat. "Echo, I think we should just drop this."

Echo reached over and touched his hand. He flinched away, but not before she flashed. *Shield Echo.*

"What's really going on?" she asked.

"Nothing," he mumbled. He glanced back down at the photo he held and shrugged, "What do I care about why Uncle Billy hid those items? Those old things don't mean anything to me."

His phone chimed, distracting him. His posture stiffened when he read the message. He took a deep breath and said, "I'd appreciate you returning the case and key to me and just forget they ever existed." Noting the stubborn set of her chin, he added, "Please."

"What are you trying to shield me from?" Echo startled him with her question. When she moved to touch him again, he shook his head and motioned with his hand for her not to come closer.

Archer sighed. He scrolled through his phone. "I received this about an hour ago. It was sent from someone calling himself *thefixer*. The sender didn't use a real name." He clicked and held his phone up for Echo to read. *Don't dig or snoopy girl gets hurt. I'll buy the case and key from you.*

"About twenty minutes later I received this." He scrolled again and showed her a second message. *$10,000. Let's swap.*

"I didn't respond so he sent this." *Be smart. Don't risk the girl. Give up the key.*

"I just don't see how any of the objects can protect or hurt anyone seventy years later. I couldn't bear someone getting hurt just to satisfy our curiosity."

"Archer, whatever the story is related to these objects,

your Uncle Billy was deeply committed to protecting something or someone. I can't make you pursue this, but you should know a menace is hanging over you and it's not going to leave just because you ignore it. There is a wave of greed linked to the key that can drag you into its undercurrent. Don't you see? Someone is rattled enough that they're making threats."

She asked, "How do we know that someone else won't get hurt if you turn over the key to this stranger?"

Archer closed his eyes, sighed and relented. "Ok. But you better be careful."

She turned to leave and had another thought, "Archer, do you have old photo albums or scrapbooks from your uncle that might give us some clues?"

He flipped his dreads off his shoulder. "I'm not sure. I have a couple boxes of stuff from my Daddy in the attic. I'd have to look through them."

"Ok. Give me a call if you find something. I'll check in with you again next week," she said.

She stepped out onto the sidewalk and paused. Tensed, her back to the store, she studied the street searching for incongruous movement or expressions. Echo shifted her bag to her back hip to keep her hands free. Extending her senses, she resumed her walk home. Someone or something was disrupting the harmony around her, but not close enough for her to get a fix on.

A few blocks further at their home, she scanned her left hand flat on the plate to unlock the front door and stepped directly into their living room. *I really love what we've done with the place,* she sang to herself. Downstairs, they had minimized the use of walls, creating an open flow with wide archways to suggest division between relaxing, eating and food prep areas. A half bath and laundry room were tucked into a back corner.

All quiet. *I might have time to wash and dry my hair before*

Hawke gets home, she thought. She crossed the hardwood floors and climbed the wood treads circling an iron center column to the second floor. *Drying these curls without creating a frizz monster is work.*

At the top of the stairs she turned right passing through the master bedroom to the ensuite bathroom. After turning on the shower, she pulled her t-shirt over her head and dropped it into the laundry bin with her pants.

"Have I seen those before?" drawled Hawke from where he lounged casually against the doorframe appreciating her slender shapely body.

"What, this old thing?" She laughed, looking down at her fiesta pink bra and panties, "OK, I admit it. I'm a lingerie junkie. Some women like shoes. Some like purses. I appreciate feminine underwear."

A tingling of excitement ran through her as he nuzzled her neck, removing the clip from her hair to release her curls. She turned into his arms, his lips parting hers in a soul-reaching massage. She murmured, "I missed you."

First he kissed her eyes, then her lips and finally, easing the lacy cup of her bra aside, his mouth touched her breast with tantalizing possessiveness. "I ached for you." His voice a velvet murmur, he slow danced her backwards. Hungry with desire, she removed her last lacy barrier while he quickly undressed.

Lowering himself to the bed over her, his hand seared a path down her abdomen to her thigh, while his tongue caressed her sensitive swollen nipples. Fire spread to her heart; she matched his urgency with her own lusty exploration of his body. She welcomed him, their bodies in exquisite harmony with each other, soaring higher until together they reached a peak, exploding in a downpour of fiery sensations.

Moments later, he wrapped his arms around Echo, gently pulling her into a sitting position with him. Twirling a lock of her hair around his finger, with a mischievous smile he chanted softly, "Firecracker, firecracker, boom, boom, boom" - a schoolgirl cheer she had teased him with as a child.

The sound of water beating on the tile wall gradually replaced the thrumming of her heart in her ears. She jumped up, smiling down at Hawke, "You're some distraction. I forgot the shower running."

"I couldn't help it. I picked up on your increased pheromones seconds after I entered the front door."

A side effect of her intuitive flashes, Echo's body incrementally released pheromones which Hawke was supersensitive to. He basked in appreciation that today her pheromones called to him like a siren. Often they activated a protection response from him – a response not always welcomed by his wife.

"We can shower together to conserve what's left of the hot water." Hawke's eyes were full of promises. "And then we can decide about dinner. I haven't eaten anything since breakfast. And I bet all you had to eat today was a granola bar."

After their shower, she dressed in a sleeveless turquoise dress, wrapped a multicolored woven belt around her waist and stepped into wedge sandals that would be comfortable for the walk. She pulled her towel-dried hair back into a low ponytail and said, "I thought we could stop at Sunset Riff after dinner. See if I can get a lead on the people in the photograph."

In casual grey slacks and a black short-sleeved shirt, Hawke waited for her at the bedroom door. "Sounds good to me. I need to catch up with Moses anyway." He mentally checked through his work projects and wondered how much interference they'd need to run with Esme. Victoria's adventurous determination exasperated her Grandmother, creating a conflict of emotions between them.

Hawke and Moses Martine shared ownership of a jazz club. Friends since grade school, Moses and Hawke had joined the army together immediately after high school. While Hawke left the armed services after two years to travel the world as a freelance photographer for National Geographic, Moses stayed for six years, the last four of them spent with the Rangers. They returned from their world adventures in the aftermath of Katrina and became business partners.

5

BOURBON STREET: *sunset riff*

Orange evolved into mauve, changed into red, faded into purple, evolved back to orange. The continuously evolving colors backlit the stained glass wall behind the bar, evoking a sunset created by the pattern of cut glass. Echo swiveled her stool, glancing around the large room from where she and Hawke sat. The musicians on the small stage were already into their second set when they arrived and all of the club chairs surrounding low tables had been occupied. A favorite of locals and popular with tourists, the Sunset Riff Jazz Club, with its art deco theme, was an intimate upscale setting on the ground floor of the Royal Sonesta Hotel. At the heart of it all on Bourbon Street, the hotel encompassed the entire frontages of Bienville, Bourbon and Conti Streets.

Contented to wait until the musicians took their next break, she sipped her Pinot Noir and listened to the soulful voice of the female in the trio. Her raw passion put a gospel and R&B hurting on the song about bad news and not sleeping at night. Next to her, Hawke and Moses' heads were bent over the bar in low conversation.

A Creole with skin the color of cane syrup, Moses' dove grey eyes looked out from a face etched with deep lines for the young age of thirty-one. Wearing his receding cinder black hair in a buzz cut, he sported a two-day stubble which leant an air of danger to him. Moses worked as a Private Investigator after leaving the Rangers, before he and Hawke opened the Sunset Riff. He kept his PI license current. It allowed him to carry a concealed weapon. And he dabbled in investigations for the Foundation which retained him on an exclusive basis. Moses affiliation with the Foundation could be a love-hate relationship. It gave Hawke and Echo's grandmother a superficial confidence in Echo's safety. But tension flared between him and Echo when she accused him of acting more like a babysitter, than an investigator. After two years of juggling his two friends' expectations, he learned to discriminate their needs and had finally settled into a compatible work relationship with each.

Most people approached the ex-Ranger with the muscled, compact build and hard bass voice cautiously. In reality, Moses had a soft spot for strays and attempted to mediate a situation before resorting to other means.

Abandoned by a teenage mother, he was raised by two aunts who attended church twice a week, starting and ending every day with a reading from the bible. Franklin "Moses" Martine got his nickname because of his fondness for quotes – from the bible and elsewhere - when trying to be the peacemaker.

Hawke and Moses - the artist and the prophet - their individual personalities blended together to create a unique space for jazz enthusiasts. Hawke designed the sunset glass behind the bar. Moses had napkins imprinted with ever changing quotes and managed the club. He often bartended, reveling in people's stories. Said he was thinking about writing a book and titling it *Has Common Sense Got Up and Walked out the Door?* Hawke sometimes sat in with musicians playing his bass guitar. Echo held up her napkin to read today's message. *When nothing goes right, go left.*

Her senses tingled, she scanned the room. *What was her mind registering that her eyes didn't see?* All the patrons appeared attentive to the musicians. The female stepped off the stage, standing to one side while the trio moved into their next number.

Echo flashed back to the photograph. *The female in the picture stood to the side of the musicians. Was she in fact a singer who performed with the group?*

During the band's next break, Moses called the musicians over to the bar and introduced Echo to them. "Echo is the CEO of the Insight Foresight Benevolent Foundation and she is working on a mystery for Archer Williams at the Museum Store." They nodded their heads indicating they knew Archer.

"You mean college boy?" The singer smiled. "Yeah. When you first see his dreads, you don't take him for a music history major. Then you only have to hear his perfect speech."

Echo held out her tablet computer, pointing her slender finger at the trumpet player in the enlarged photograph. "That's his uncle. Do any of you have an idea who the people with Billy Williams might be?" she asked.

"Oh, man those guys are too old for me to know," the young drummer said.

The pianist, who appeared to be in his early fifties, scrutinized the picture. "I don't recognize any of them, but you might ask Maurice Jones. His daddy, Cap Jones, played with Billy back in the day. And the piano player maybe resembles Maurice a little."

Excited, Echo asked, "How can I contact Maurice? Is he local?"

"I don't have his phone number." He hurriedly added, seeing Echo's obvious disappointment, "But I hear he's supposed to be playing horn at St. Augustine's Jazz Mass on Sunday."

Echo showed the musicians and Moses a photograph of the cigarette case and key. "Does this monogram *TMS* mean anything to you?"

"No."

"Nada."

"Unh, unh." The singer shook her head side to side then pointed to the key. "Pretty design. What does it go to?"

"I wish I knew," replied Echo.

The young drummer piped up, "Too small for a door. Too large for a diary. Could open a box or trunk or something like that."

"Time for us to do our final set," the pianist turned back to the stage area, signaling for the others to join him.

Echo placed her hand on the pianist's arm, stilling his movement."One last question. Do any of you recognize the club in this picture?"

His head cocked to the side, the guitar player said, "A couple of places on Bourbon Street have wooden wall panels like that. You know, the Preservation Hall has a photo archive. You might find a match looking through them."

The pianist called back, "Good luck with your hunt."

"What's so special about that picture and them items?" asked a thin man who sat on the stool next to Echo. He indicated the tablet lying on the bar in front of Echo.

"A friend of mine discovered them when his uncle's house was demolished. He's interested in understanding their significance – curious about why they were hidden."

"Seems like old news to me. Who cares?" His pressed lips turned up but his sharp and assessing eyes contradicted his simulated smile.

34

Echo lifted her chin and boldly met his gaze. "Someone is more than a little interested since they tried to steal these items. I care because my friend's business was trashed and he could have been hurt. And he was threatened!"

He coughed. "I just meant those people are probably dead or very old. And those items don't exactly look like valuable antiques." With a slight smirk, he said, "Seems like this mystery may be a tad exaggerated."

The man leaned closer, the smell of his cologne unpleasantly strong. "Why you got a photograph? Where are the real items?"

"They're in a safe place." Echo's senses buzzed, the air around her turning muddy. She extended her hand, introducing herself to the stranger, "Hi, I'm Echo LeBauve. Are you local or visiting our Crescent City?"

His head jerked back slightly, eyes rounded – startled that she was waiting for him to introduce himself. Clearing his throat, he shook her hand briefly, "Larry Nash. I work here in New Orleans but this is my first time at the Sunset Riff. Lovely place. He placed money on the bar for his tab, standing up. "Good meeting you, Echo, but I have to run." And he walked out.

Echo looked up to see that Moses had observed her exchange with the man. "My senses were strumming when I touched his hand – grey storm cloud but no distinct images. What do you think?"

"A little too interested in making you believe old news is no news," said Moses.

"Ever see him in here before?"

"Not that I recall." He held up a napkin to show he had written down the man's name. "I'll work with Zetta to find any background on him, just in case."

A gentle nudge distracted her. Hawke turned her stool to face him. He arched one eyebrow inquiringly, "Ready to go

35

home?"

"Hmmm?" She tore her mind away from thoughts of the stranger. "Yes."

Hawke intertwined his fingers in hers, holding hands, as they walked home. Such an old fashioned gesture, but a warm glow flowed through her at his touch. "Instead of our regular mass, how do you feel about attending St. Augustine's Jazz Mass on Sunday?" She had no idea how sensuous her voice sounded.

A smile ruffled his mouth, he shrugged matter-of-factly. "I already anticipated you, sweetheart. Moses will meet us there at ten-thirty, early enough for us to find a seat. But, in the meantime, let's enjoy tomorrow."

He was still perfecting the choreography between supporting and protecting his spirited wife.

♫♪

Tick. Tock. Tick. Tock. Tick. The ticking, which sounded like one finger alternately tapping a sharp and flat piano key, came from a clock floating in the background, zooming in and out of focus. A treble clef swung in place of a pendulum. The row of stools shaped like fat flowers standing under the clock was stalked by a man bird. The gooney bird with a man's face and wheels in place of feet rolled back and forth, silent.

She asked the man bird, "What are you doing?"

He squawked, "I'm watching for you."

"Why?"

He flapped his wings, speeded up his trundling and said, "To tell me which of these flowers hides my master's treasure."

Echo guided her subconscious out of slumber, back to reality - aware she was dreaming. Although she had inherited the Leger trait of foretelling dreams, her sleeping thoughts were more like visiting Tim Burton's adaptation of Alice's

Wonderland. She had not mastered the art of interpreting their meaning. Since they usually made sense after the fact she had learned to be wary and extra observant following slumber visited by the fanciful creations of her imagination.

When they were children, Victoria revealed her fear that predictive dreams would mean dreadful thoughts and visions. Hawke had appeared the next day with a dream catcher. He handed the woven twigs and string decorated with feathers and glass beads to Victoria saying, "Hang this dream net where you sleep. It sifts your dreams, allowing good imaginings to slip through." Because she had her first vivid dream that night, Echo credited the net for filtering out the frightful and snaring the bizarre, colorful imagery her mind conjured up.

What kind of flowers were those stools she wondered, drifting back into a restful sleep.

6

DOWNTOWN: *the partner*

Early Saturday morning, the restaurant was not yet crowded. An unlikely couple to meet for breakfast – the serious young professor-like and older gregarious businessman selected a table away from the other customers. The slender man relaxed into a chair across from his breakfast companion. "On your way to a golf game?" he asked, indicating the monogrammed golf shirt the older man wore.

The shirt was a favorite. It fit his thick chest and shoulders so well - even if the monogram was a little pretentious. With an absent smile, he said. "Yes. A birthday gift from my wife. I have a late tee off." He fiddled with his silverware aligning the bottom edges on the tablecloth. Lowering his voice he said, "My partner is acting paranoid."

"Do you think he suspects you?"

Shaking his head, the businessman said, "I don't believe his paranoia is aimed at me, but I'm not sure." He frowned in concentration. "Something else. He was rattled when he arrived at the office yesterday and he kept his door closed. I could hear him talking to someone, but the light wasn't lit on our office phone. He must have been using his cell phone."

"Ok. I'll ask the others on our team if they've picked up any scuttlebutt. So what's on your schedule next with him?"

"Since we're representing the City Council at White Linen Night, we agreed to each take one side of the street to cover all of the galleries. I won't be able to tell you much of who he meets or talks with tonight."

The slender man motioned to the waiter for their check, nudging his glasses back into position. "I'll take care of that. Anything else?"

"Yes. He insisted I attend the St. Augustine Jazz Mass with him and another councilman tomorrow. Said it was a great opportunity to get more exposure." He stared earnestly at the man across from him. "It just doesn't ring true. He enjoys the role of grand politician and it's highly unusual for him to share the limelight."

The studious looking man polished his glasses while he considered how to handle Sunday. "Well, I don't think we can conjure up a reason for me to accompany you without causing suspicion. I'll put a couple of my men in and outside of the church. If he directs the driver on any side trips, you can text me."

7

Backyard: *poppy's perspective*

Morning sunlight peeping through the balcony doors tripped her eyelids open. All quiet except for the drone of the ceiling fan. Alone in bed. She hadn't heard Hawke leave to finish last minute preparations for his gallery show tonight.

She showered, pulled on cotton shorts and a t-shirt, finger combed her tousled curls and headed down the circular staircase.

A torn piece of cardboard sat propped in front of her favorite tea mug on the counter with a firecracker drawn in the center of a heart. *You are my Heart. Will be home after lunch.* The handwritten note was signed simply *H*.

Happiness filled her. She thanked the divine providence at play when Hawke entered her life. When they had announced their engagement, Hawke and Echo watched in disbelief when Poppy walked out of the room without comment. Just when their anxiety about his departure started to escalate, he returned, handing them a drawing with his blessing. "I've been waiting for this moment to give this to you.

Individually, you are intelligent, creative, and courageous. Together, you are electric harmony intertwined with faith and trust."

As she steeped a tea bag, she studied the frame with Poppy's drawing on the kitchen counter next to the back door. The crayon drawing resembled a child's rendition of a stick figure man and woman with messy coloring outside of the lines. A blue hue surrounded Hawke while Echo was emblazoned by gold. Poppy said the green arch connecting their heads represented their intellectual attunement and harmony. Pink encircled their hearts showing love. A scarlet red lightning bolt fringed with ruby pink joined the two figures. Echo smiled at Poppy's artistic dramatization of their strong passions, willpowers and convictions.

Poppy had 'the touch'. Although he sometimes had predictive dreams, Poppy's gift was seeing auras which helped him heal others. He said the hazy bubble of lights that surround an individual gave him an instant insight into their personality, their true nature and pointed to their future destiny. According to Poppy, the indigo blue that ringed Hawke's head indicated he was calm, sensitive and creative. The deep red at his shoulders meant he was grounded, strong-willed and survival-oriented.

Through the screen door she spotted her grandfather tending lemon, lime and orange trees which he had trained in espalier fashion along the western fence. Mastering espalier technique involves understanding how the plant responds to pruning cuts and shape manipulation. Poppy had chosen the buds he wanted to form into branches on a two rail fence like the one in Monet's garden, cultivating them with a patient, curative touch.

The fragrant flowers of spring had bloomed into full-size fruit along the flat planes of branch. The citrus would mature over the next several months, their green skins ripening to yellow. It is said that Monet would not have become the painter he became if he wasn't the gardener he was. Echo believed the reverse was true for Poppy. Poppy's healing gift extended to vitalizing plants – evidenced by the exceptionally healthy trees bearing fruit in abundance on which fungus didn't dare intrude.

Poppy lived in the other half of their shotgun house. Their shared back yard extended their living space. Personalized areas of sanctuary created a distinctive courtyard microcosm.

At the far end of the deep but narrow lot sat a shallow out building. Separate entrances gave Hawke and Poppy their own workshops. Glass paneled doors and skylights provided plenty of natural light.

Out the door and down the steps, past the last of summer's tomatoes and peppers growing in above-ground vegetable garden squares, she plucked a cherry tomato still damp with morning dew, popped it into her mouth and smacked her lips, savoring the flavor. Steadying her mug of tea in her left hand, she leaned down to where her grandfather knelt in the garden, giving him a one arm hug. "Good morning, Poppy."

The moss separating the pave stones felt cool to her bare feet. Crossing the yard, she sat at the edge of a small pond. She often practiced her tai chi in this refuge spot. The hypnotizing sound of the water spray and sight of gold fish swimming between rocks and bog plants invited reflection.

Poppy tilted his head back looking up from under the brim of his worn and stained plantation straw hat. He still wore his hair in a long plait, its red now faded to a lighter strawberry color. "Mornin' Shǎ. What are you musing on today?"

After hearing about Archer's mystery, he commented, "Whatever information was hidden by Billy Williams is now seventy to seventy-five years old. Probably all of the people in the photograph are dead by now so it couldn't hurt them."

Echo shook her head in agreement. "That's what Mr. Cologne Man said last night. And unless the key opens a treasure chest full of money, I don't think anyone tried to steal those items because of their value."

"Yeah, well, that's exactly what a blogger this morning is speculating about – what kind of treasure the key leads to." Poppy shook his head in wonderment. "We have many value systems, Shǎ." He sat on his haunch wiping his face with a faded bandana. "Ethical, moral, economic, doctrinal, social, intrinsic." He paused, "You get my drift. Individuals rank values differently. Which value is driving your mystery person – inducing his behavior?"

Echo pounced on Poppy's comment, her voice trembling with excitement. "Treasure! Why am I so inept at interpreting my dreams. Last night a manbird visited me. He haunted these big fat flowers and said something about hiding his master's treasure. I think the crazy tick-tock warned me that something is looming."

She nudged the cool moss with her bare toes while she mulled over the dream. "The flowers were a caricature of the real thing. I keep thinking I should know what kind of flowers they were – that it's significant."

Continuing to work through her dream aloud, she said, "Someone is worried about a long-hidden fact becoming public. They have something to protect, their treasure, so to speak."

His blue eyes thoughtful, Poppy said, "There's no accounting for some people's perspective of reputation. Consider how your Grandmother Esme frets that your work – or antics as she calls them – will cause harmful publicity for the family reputation. Maybe you should look for relatives of people in that picture. The question is how can it harm them now?"

"Archer is a relative and has no idea about the meaning of those items. But, we do have a lead on a possible relative of another person in the photo. We're going to the Jazz Mass tomorrow to see if we can speak with him."

8

THE WAREHOUSE DISTRICT: *white linen night*

The brassy timbre of horns and mellow warmth plucked from bass strings floated in through the Horizon Gallery's open door. Crowds of people strolled up and down Julia Street, stepping in and out of art galleries, most of them dressed in shades of white. Some carried glasses of wine and munched finger food. White Linen Night in New Orleans is one of the summer's biggest block parties featuring a tour of galleries in the Warehouse Arts District, with food, music and special exhibitions. Tourists milled with locals mixing elegance with fun during the Saturday night event of the Louis Armstrong Festival weekend.

The centerpiece of Hawke LeBauve's *Reflections* Exhibit displayed in a double frame on a tripod and entitled *Sunset, Sunrise* was not for sale. A twelve year old Hawke had raised his camera, capturing a dancing nine year old Echo in the rich sunset reflected on the muddy water of the Bayou Teche. The setting sun stained the air a red-orange-purple slush causing

Victoria's messy curls to blaze with fiery highlights – a mini explosion of ginger and silver.

Eighteen years later while Echo sat barefoot in a canoe dressed only in a peach slip with tousled hair, Hawke photographed *Sunrise*. Yellows and pinks colored the air surrounding her as the sun nudged its way up from the riverbank. Then he proposed to her.

In the spirit of White Linen Night Echo wore white even though it wasn't the most flattering color for her alabaster skin. A college friend building a reputation as a dressmaker designed her dress- a sleeveless, pencil dress fitted to her slim waist - calling it romantic elegant. A fitted heart shaped neckline and bodice kept the design youthful and a tiny aqua green cord woven through the waistline accentuated a small waist, adding a touch of color to the white pique. She had tamed her red curls back into a chignon. The strappy heels matched the color of the cord and added at least two inches to her five foot eight inch height, so tonight her chin reached above Hawke's shoulder. Even though she felt elegant at this moment, she knew the closer she got to the open door and humidity outside, her curls would start escaping from the knot at her nape.

"Stunning." Hawke brushed his lips across the back of Echo's neck.

Accepting the glass of red wine offered by her husband, Echo leaned her head against his shoulder murmuring "Yes. Hawke, your exhibit is getting such positive attention tonight. I think it tops your last exhibit, *Rain*."

Hawke traced his finger lightly down the side of Echo's face, whispering, "I meant you." His liquid brown eyes promised an intimacy which was only theirs. Casual and elegant in cream linen pants and shirt, tonight his hair swung loose sweeping his chin. The hook in his nose and serious expression gave him a somewhat regal air.

"Cut it out, you two. You're in public." They turned toward the deep voice. Both Moses and Zetta had scorned the dress code. Zetta's flaring pink and red rose printed skirt blatantly disregarded the "white rule" while Moses khaki pants and light almond shirt hinted at his disrespect.

With a slight curtsy and regal sweep of her hand, Zetta said, "I'm betting tomorrow's T-P is Mr. and Mrs. Elegant." When creating an online scrapbook for the Foundation, Zetta noticed a trend and categorized the descriptions of Echo and Hawke written in the news. It soon became a tally game. Besides Mr. and Mrs. Elegant, her most common monikers were Mr. and Mrs. Exotic, Mr. and Mrs. Benevolent, Mr. Talented and Mrs. Escapade.

The Mrs. Escapade moniker introduced itself when the newspaper reported Echo's adventures during a mystery investigation as front page news, exposing a local businessman's illegal gun running sideline. Not exactly fond of Echo's previous job as an investigative reporter, Grandmother Esme found the publicity typically associated with the Mrs. Escapade category even more distasteful. Echo avoided discussing the Foundation's mystery work with her grandmother, dreading the tension it inevitably caused.

Zetta changed subjects, taking a cue from Echo's frowning expression. She pointed her thumb in the direction of the doorway, eyes laughing through her red framed glasses, "Poppy Rouge is holding court outside in the street. A line seems to be forming. Word must have spread that he's reading auras."

"I hope some of them realize it's not a parlor game and take advantage of his insights," said Moses.

Barricades blocked street traffic for the night and temporary music stages had been erected in the center of Julia Street. Park benches and music encouraged patrons to relax and mingle between gallery tours.

Outside, Rouge Leger sat on one of the benches at the center of a small group – probably tourists. His white straw hat topped an outfit of white shirt, white shorts and his old white mesh slip-on boat shoes. When Echo had cocked her head in question at his dress earlier tonight, he shrugged, "What? It's ninety-eight degrees outside. I'm white, but I'm cool. Besides, Shă," he teased, "I don't have to concern myself with being featured in the newspaper."

She threw her head back and laughed, knowing Moses and Zetta loved Rouge. "The gallery owners probably didn't realize they would get free entertainment tonight. Isn't it convenient that he parked himself right outside of the gallery featuring Hawke?"

"On a more sober note, I just saw that skinny man from the bar out there," Moses said. "He's driving a silver town car. Stopped at the corner and got out to open the back door for his passenger.

"Mr. Cologne Larry Nash?" asked Echo. She had picked up Zetta's habit of assigning descriptive monikers to people.

"Yep," said Zetta. I snapped a picture of him. I didn't find anything relevant in a quick Google search, so I remoted in and started other searches running. He doesn't look like a social network kind of guy, but you never know about people." She held out her smart phone to show Echo a snapshot. "Do you know his passenger?"

"No, I don't recognize him," replied Echo.

A quiet, cultured voice interrupted them, "Hawke, your work reveals a very sensitive man. Your photographic centerpiece captures the essence of Victoria – fire, spirit and muse." Esme Delahaye, her classic blonde beauty still evident at age seventy-seven, wore a white silk pant suit and a strand of large round pearls - their rose overtone adding the only color besides her lipstick.

Echo hugged her, air kissing each cheek careful not to

smudge her grandmother's perfect make-up. "Grandmother Esme, we're so happy to see you. We weren't sure you'd make the drive across the lake at night."

"That's what I have a driver for, child," said Esme, her voice lacking any inflection of humor. Realizing she may have sounded a bit haughty, she smiled and said in a lighter tone, "And since I'm not driving, I'm allowed a glass of wine which an acquaintance of mine is fetching for me."

Esme focused her attention on the centerpiece duet. "I especially like how you printed those photographs on canvass."

From the far side of the room the Gallery owner, Elaine, motioned Hawke over to where a patron was admiring the close-up photograph of a red bird reflected in a woman's blue iris. "Excuse me. Business calls," said Hawke. Before he stepped away from the group, he kissed Esme on the cheek saying, "Thank you for attending my exhibition."

"White wine, as you requested, dear Esme." A stout man of average height with wispy sandy brown hair combed across his balding top joined the group, handing a glass to Esme. Adhering strictly to the white dress code, he wore white oxford shoes and a white sports coat with a monogrammed white handkerchief peeking out of his breast pocket.

Zetta averted her face and took a gulp of her wine to disguise her snicker at the man's pretentious garb. Echo could only imagine what label Zetta was mentally tagging him with.

After handing Esme her wine, the man used his handkerchief to wipe perspiration from his florid face. The gallery was air conditioned, but with the door propped open, it was warm to be wearing a sports jacket.

"Sorry, I was delayed." Esme's companion looked back to where Hawke was talking with a prospective buyer and announced, "I had difficulty choosing between the *Robin in the Iris* and the *Flower in the Raindrop*. I finally decided on the raindrop for the reception area of my office."

"It's one of my favorites. Catching a raindrop in midair was a stupendous shot," Echo said with obvious pride. "The photograph is from Hawke's *Rain* collection and gave my husband the idea for this *Reflections* series."

Esme thanked him for the wine and introduced Echo to the man. "Teddy, this is my granddaughter, Victoria LeBauve." She explained by way of introducing him to the others, "Teddy Stanton and I have served on several committees together." She looked around the gallery and asked, "Is Catherine with you?"

"No. My partner and I agreed to attend sans wives tonight. Between the many social and political obligations, I'm afraid our wives sometimes view it as a burden."

"Any connection to Stanton and Silverman Commercial Properties?" Zetta asked Teddy in her forthright manner.

He responded with a humble brag, "Yes. It's my company."

"Looks like you're our landlord, then," said Zetta.

Confused, Teddy asked "Our?"

Echo introduced Zetta and Moses as the CFO and sometimes Private Investigator of the Foundation. "The Insight Foresight Benevolent Foundation leases one of your properties in that cozy alleyway off Royal."

Putting his handkerchief away in his jacket pocket, Teddy shook hands with Zetta and Moses with the usual pleasantry, "Good to meet you."

He clasped Echo's hand between his clammy palms saying, "I heard a little about your foundation, but must admit it's an unusual name and I don't really understand what you do."

FLASH! *Obsessed with Property.*

I wonder if his business is in jeopardy due to the recent economic downturn? With a slight quick shake to clear her head, she pulled her hand away. Her bright emerald eyes directed at him, she said sweetly, "It's simple, Mr. Stanton. Our mission is to find inventive and effective means to help people help themselves."

Teddy drew his shoulders back, puffing his chest out slightly. "I don't mean to sound disheartening, but that sounds so ideological. In my experience that's harder to do than say."

Moses coughed to hide his amusement. Echo's sweet eyes turned flinty. He anticipated a rapid fire spiel from her. In his resonant deep voice, he teased, "Here it comes."

"Although we support meaningful traditional programs, the Insight Foresight Foundation's benevolence focuses on experimenting with variations which may prove to be more effective."

Her chin set in a stubborn line, self-confidence vibrating; she spoke eagerly, "That probably still sounds too idealistic, so here are a few real examples of our programs to demonstrate."

"The Foundation sponsors several music programs for children. We work with schools and volunteers to give instruments and music lessons to children because it's been scientifically proven that learning to read music can increase intelligence. It stimulates both sides of the brain and improves your memory.

Pride kept her going, "In fact, one of our children's groups is performing Sunday on the Satchmo Festival stage."

"We support a communal living model for the elderly that relies less on paid assistants. The model combines organizational features from both communal and assisted living communities. We actually learned more than free love from the counterculture commune movement of the sixties and seventies."

Esme's posture stiffened.

Echo gently nudged her grandmother with her shoulder, ligtening her tone, "We've partnered with the Delahaye School of Etiquette and Protocol to bring social skills to less advantaged students because manners and etiquette are closely related to self-confidence. Mastering important life skills can help a person triumph with self-assurance."

She took a deep breath, knowing she had pushed the envelope of what Grandmother Esme believed to be graceful etiquette, sipped her wine and curbed her determination to convince Mr. Stanton that the Foundation's mission wasn't unrealistic. She said, "The Foundation also invests in start-up technologies which assist handicapped individuals."

"Fascinating work. You're a very passionate advocate for your Foundation." He retained affability, but with a hint of mocking he asked, "Are you this passionate about the other line of work the Foundation conducts? I believe you refer to it as solving mysteries."

Uh-oh. It was obvious from Esme's thin smile, taut expression and the pulsating vein on her thin neck that her grandmother was unhappy with where this discussion was heading. Moses and Zetta were familiar with the signs. Esme's Miss Disdain was about to appear.

Ever the mediator, Moses tried to discourage any further conversation about mysteries. His deep voice like a marshmallow melting in steaming hot chocolate, he said, "Mr. Stanton, mysteries are a small part of what our Foundation does. And we approach all of our projects with zeal, fidelity and discretion."

Undeterred, Teddy pushed the subject, "Victoria, I am captivated by your zest- the way you champion your Foundation's work. Is it true that you think you found a mystery at the Museum Store?"

Moses took one step forward, his congenial expression turning stony, ready to ward off Stanton's preoccupation with their mystery work. Zetta touched Esme's elbow, gently guiding her away from the group, "Why don't you and I go find another glass of wine and a more entertaining conversation?"

Echo sighed in relief. She loved her grandmother dearly, but this was one area where they clashed, each of them stubborn in their viewpoints. To keep the peace, Zetta, Hawke and Moses had become experts in diverting and distracting Esme away from mysteries. *I'm not a coward, but it's just easier to deal with after. And who knows, maybe this mystery won't result in headline news.*

She touched Teddy's arm by way of apology, her tone with quiet emphasis, "I'm sorry, Mr. Stanton. My grandmother doesn't appreciate my involvement in mysteries, so we try to protect her from the detail."

FLASH. Cloudy mushroom whirled in her mind. *Dissatisfaction. Was Mr. Stanton dwelling on his property concern or was he dissatisfied with something she said?*

Ping, Ping. Ping, Ping. Across the room, the gallery owner tapped her gemstone ring against her wine glass to get everyone's attention. Elaine stood with Hawke next to the *Sunset, Sunrise* double frame resting on a tripod floor easel.

"I'd like to present a toast before we close the exhibit," raising her glass to Hawke. "Congratulations to Hawke LeBauve for another amazingly creative photographic series."

"Here, here," chorused the patrons.

Elaine raised her glass in toast first indicating the *Sunset, Sunrise* photographs, then waved toward Echo. "And to Hawke's muse, his beautiful wife, Victoria."

One of the guests called out, "To Hawke and his muse."

Hawke winked at Echo. His expression then stilled and shifted into mellow satisfaction. Slowly and confidently taking in each patron with his magnetic brown eyes, he spoke in a low, composed voice. "I am humbled by the support and encouragement I receive for my art and I sincerely thank each of you for your patronage tonight."

Rejoining Echo after the applause ended, Hawke tipped his glass towards her grandmother at the center of an animated group across the room and commented, "Esme stayed out late tonight."

She looked up at him, amusement flickering in her eyes. "I ruffled her feathers when I showed a little too much enthusiasm for talking about the Foundation. With a self-deprecating giggle she said, "She probably stayed as a silent reminder to behave myself like a lady."

His left eyebrow rose a fraction, "Say goodnight to your grandmother and I'll escort her to her driver. Then we can wrap up here and go home."

Moses rushed up to them, "The alarm just went off at the office. I'm leaving to check it out.

"What happ…?"

Before Echo could finish her question, Moses said, "I don't know anything else," And turned to leave. He called over his shoulder, "Will check in with you after I inspect the place."

Hawke and Echo joined Esme and Zetta. "Boss, the .."

Echo interrupted, her eyes warning Zetta not to say more in front of Esme. "We know. Moses is on his way." She turned to hug her grandmother good night.

FLASH. *Pink, the color of mother love.* The familiar sweet fragrance had a cool tranquil effect, transporting her back to a moment when her grandmother had rocked her in her lap on her lakefront porch idly watching the sailboats tack in lazy loops on Lake Pontchartrain. If only she could hold on to this feeling. Her relationship with her grandmother was complicated by conflicting emotions and warring personas. Echo whispered a heartfelt, "I love you. Thank you, Grandmother, for coming tonight."

Raising her voice to include the others, she said, "Since the street is blocked off, Hawke will walk you safely to your car and driver."

Esme said to Zetta, "Thank you for your company tonight young lady." Before walking out with Hawke, Esme kissed Echo on the cheek saying, "Goodnight, Victoria. I'll see you on Monday afternoon for your etiquette class."

When Echo had persuaded her grandmother to collaborate with the Foundation, Esme stipulated that Echo must personally present one of the program's seminars on behalf of the Delahaye Etiquette School. In their ongoing dance of the stubborn, Echo designed her seminar to demonstrate how a young person could maintain etiquette without becoming a milquetoast.

After Hawke escorted Esme out, Zetta said to Echo in a hushed tone, "The alarm at the office was triggered by tampering, but there's no indication that anyone broke into the space."

Echo asked Zetta, "Are the cigarette case and key in the safe?"

"I locked them away before I left yesterday. Do you think that's what this is about?"

Echo responded, "I can't think of any other reason anyone would try to break in, except to steal all that fancy equipment you have. I bet they didn't count on that super security system you installed. Can't cut the telephone wires like they did at Archer's store."

♫♪

A young man in blue uniform stood outside the wrought iron fence. Moses parked behind the police car, with its light bar on the roof silently rotating between red and blue. He jumped out of the car and strode towards the gates guarding the Foundation's courtyard.

The policeman pointed to the locked gates, "I couldn't get any closer to the buildings to check out the alarm so I searched the immediate vicinity when I arrived. Didn't find anyone or anything suspicious."

Moses acknowledged the policeman with a nod, moving closer to the gates. He inspected the keyhole with a flashlight, confirming the gates were indeed locked with no obvious signs of forcing the lock. He paced, looking closely for signs of disturbance on the moss covered brick base of the wrought iron fence on either side of the gate.

He returned to the policeman. "The triggered alarm came from our front door scan system." Looking up at the finial points atop the eight foot high fence, Moses said, "This gate and fence isn't on our alarm system, but the person or persons had to get past it into the courtyard somehow."

"Yeah, probably jumped the fence," said the officer.

He unlocked the gates with his key, inviting the policeman in. While the patrolman inspected the courtyard for signs of intruders, Moses shined his flashlight on the scan plate next to the Foundation's front door. Scratch marks on the face and sides indicated tampering, but the scanner looked undamaged.

Scanning his hand, he unlocked the door and flipped the lights on, his eyes quickly sweeping the space. Nothing looked disturbed. He walked to the center of the room and lifted the woven rag rug beneath the cedar table revealing a floor safe. Keying in the combination, he opened the safe, confirming the cigarette case and key were still secure.

"No obvious damage or intrusion to any of the three businesses in this courtyard." The policeman whistled when he scanned the interior from where he stood in the doorway. "Never seen an office look like this. Maybe they were hoping to loot some of your high tech stuff."

The safe door clicked shut. Moses dropped the rug back into position and stood, brushing any dust off the knees of his pants. He didn't see how the policeman could assist further. "Thank you, Officer, for the prompt response. Nothing seems to be missing or damaged."

After he ushered the policeman back to his cruiser, he locked up the office and relocked the gates thinking *"This was an amateur attempt to breach our security system, but he either climbed over an eight foot fence or had a key to the gate."*

Before driving away, he sent a text message to Echo and Zetta. When her phone vibrated on their short drive home, Echo read Moses' text aloud to Hawke and Poppy, "All is ok at the office and items intact in the safe."

Poppy leaned forward in the back seat and tapped Hawke on the shoulder to get his attention. "Son, what are you upset about?"

Rattled by Poppy's question and anxious she had overlooked something significant on her husband's special night, Echo faced his side profile. "Oh Hawke, is something wrong?" When she spoke, it was like champagne lava flowing.

"Shsh," he calmed her. "Nothing is wrong. I'm not upset about anything."

"That dingy pumpkin color bubbling around your head says you're fighting for self-control." Poppy quietly insisted.

"Ok, OK," Hawke laughed. "Here I was, very proud of my restraint – in not demanding Victoria keep Moses involved in her investigation."

"Demand?" Echo asked. Ice-skating violins chased the champagne out of her voice. "Keep Moses close to me now for what? To protect me from a sloppy thief?"

Hawke's jaw tensed in stubborness, "To quote your beloved Dr. Seuss, *It's not about what it is, it's about what it can become.*"

Echo decided it wasn't a good time to share the precognition of danger she had experienced in Archer's store. She let her voice melt back into lava, "Haven't I kept my promise to you? No reckless conduct. I admit that sometimes I still struggle to curb my impetuousness."

Wanting to maintain levity, she referred to a time when

her impulsive behavior had tried the patience of the good nuns of Holy Rosary Academy. "I haven't painted my hair with green and orange Jell-O for years."

Hawke reached out and caught her hand in his, an enigmatic expression on his face. He allowed her to believe she distracted him with her voice and wit.

Poppy popped his head over the front seat to look at Hawke's chest. "Orange red. You're channeling your energy back to passion. That's my boy!"

♫♫

The trumpet player sat across the chess board from an older man dressed in a suit. They stared at each other, neither making a move. A piano player fiddled with his black and white ivories. Tick. Tock. The drummer joined, alternating between his snare and bass pedal. Tick. Tock.

A girl, younger than the men, danced impatiently around the chess players. "Let's play something else."Excited, she tossed something at the trumpet player and called, "Hot Potato."

The trumpet player tossed it to the drummer who immediately got rid of it to the piano player. Man bird rolled in, flapped his wings at the musicians and chased the object. The only one who could see her, the trumpet player asked her, "Aren't you going to play?"

Echo awoke. She drank in the comfort of Hawke's nearness as she contemplated the floodtide of her mind. After a tempestuous lovemaking, the pulse at her husband's throat beat strong even as he slept. The turbulence of their passion still swirled, yet peace again flowed between them.

What was the object man bird chased?

9

UPTOWN: *after*

The cigar tip glowed red. His boss had remained silent, in a slow fume, since Nash had collected him from the gallery. The businessman in the back seat of the silver sedan took angry puffs before he finally spoke. "Did anyone see you?"

Larry Nash made an effort to keep his voice neutral and reassuring. "I don't think so. One police car arrived, but he didn't venture far away from the entrance. Stayed there until that Creole Moses showed up, and then they inspected the courtyard and went inside the Foundation office."

"Were you able to find anything?" barked the man.

Forgetting his intent to remain calm, Nash let his anger interfere and retorted, "Man, they have a very sophisticated, sealed security system. No one is breaking into that place by cutting wires."

The man in the back seat harrumphed, "Well we'll just have to find a way to get to the objects before they lock up, or provoke her into bringing them out."

Nash pulled the car into the driveway of the uptown mansion, adjusting the rearview mirror to look at his boss in the back seat. His eyebrows knotted. Through clenched teeth he said, "That Moses guy was inspecting the gate lock and fence real close. What if he suspects you?"

The man rejected the thought with contempt. "He has no reason to suspect me. Can you imagine how many keys to that gate my partner and agents of our firm have given out over the last forty years?" He stepped out of the automobile without saying goodnight to his driver.

10

TREME: *jazz mass*

Located in the Treme neighborhood of New Orleans the property was once part of a plantation estate subdivided into lots sold to free people of color. Unremarkable in its simple rectangle design, less than two feet of lawn separated the building frontage from the sidewalk on Gov. Nicholls Street. Copper brown rust streaked down the white stone exterior from small metal framed windows built high into the walls. The essence of St. Augustine Church was not in its architecture, but in its continuing history.

A few months before the dedication of St. Augustine Church in 1842, the people of color began to purchase pews for their families to sit. The War of the Pews began when white people in the area started a campaign to buy more pews than the colored folks. Ultimately won by the free people of color who bought three pews to everyone purchased by whites, the mix of the pews resulted in the most integrated congregation in the entire country.

Door stops propped the heavy wooden doors open to accommodate the early crowd. Echo accepted a hand fan from an usher welcoming visitors to the church. A local funeral home which sponsored the Jazz Mass and second line parade advertised below the Guardian Angel imprinted on the bread-slice-shaped paperboard. Reminiscent of the days before air conditioning, the stick handled paper fan actually did provide relief from hot stuffiness like today in old buildings with ineffective cooling systems.

Hawke and Echo arrived early enough to find seats in one of the side pews which, historians reported, had been given to slaves as their exclusive place of worship, a first in the history of slavery in the United States. In an unprecedented social, political and religious move, during the War of the Pews the colored members also bought all the pews of both side aisles.

The empty pews filled fast while the musicians set up in the north transept of the church. In the final fifteen minutes before mass, conversation hummed around them. Early arrivals shifted to make room for newcomers to sit. As many people attended this mass for the Brass Band show as did for spiritual worship. But it was a helpful fundraising opportunity for the beleaguered parish which still struggled with building repairs needed since Hurricane Katrina.

Popular with tourists, whether Catholic or not, the Jazz Mass with its spiritually evocative music, had become a tradition on the last day of the SummerFest celebrating Louis Armstrong's birthday.

Echo asked Hawke in a loud whisper. "I wonder which one is Maurice?"

"He's the one in the bright yellow suit playing cornet." Dressed in khaki shorts like many of the tourists waiting for mass to begin, Moses slid into the pew next to Echo. He pointed to a light black, bald man who looked to be in his mid fifties settling into one of the folding chairs at the left side of the crossing. "I met him outside and he's willing to talk with us after mass."

The musicians stood, their instruments readied. The crowd shushed in anticipation. Brass notes opened the mass with a processional hymn. Everyone rose for the entrance of the priest and deacon, sitting again after the opening prayer. The non-Catholic tourists copied the parishioners' movements.

Today's ceremony used every possible opportunity to showcase music causing the service to last longer than the normal sixty minutes. Echo enjoyed the ritual of a Sunday mass finding it a soothing backdrop to her reflections. She and Hawke usually attended church at St Louis Cathedral with Poppy; but excited about her first Jazz Mass experience, she let her eyes and mind wander. The 'All-Seeing Eye' prominent in the round window looking down onto St. Augustine's main altar was a bit disconcerting. A stained glass rendition of St. Clothilde ministering to the poor and suffering seemed more appropriate for a church.

The 'Alleluia', sung by a choir, announced the gospel with the best horn players of the Vieux Care. Like a jazz theme, each musician showcased his skills in a solo moment playing his best for God and Satchmo. The acclamation ended in a high crescendo, with the choir, horns, drums and bass moving the entire audience to some higher plane.

The young Philippine priest stood in the center of the crossing to give his Homily. He was difficult to understand, his diction unclear, often dropping the hard consonant at the end of a word. His commentary rambled, probably excited to have a large audience. The 'Alleluia' was a hard act to follow. Echo thought the choir and musicians probably came close to the seraphim and cherubim when they sang their alleluia to the shepherds at Christ's birth.

Echo's mind wandered again. Her own personal relationship with God was an ongoing conversation - not a focus on abstract rules or doctrine. She learned tolerance and respect from Poppy for all faiths.

The powerful blare of the horns drew her attention back to the mass. She and Hawke joined the congregation making their way to communion. Moses stayed seated since he was Baptist. They moved slowly in line towards the altar, as pews emptied and refilled with the communicants. Echo spotted Sal Bertucci and his wife, Bella, returning to their pew. She smiled, waving one finger to silently say hi. Bella winked, but Sal seemed distracted, not acknowledging her.

Barely had the priest given the final blessing, closing the ceremony, before the musicians broke into a rousing rendition of "The Saints Go Marching In". Decorated umbrellas popped open and handkerchiefs waved above heads of the visitors following the procession out the doors. They spilled out into the street where marching clubs in colorful costumes milled around waiting for the crowd to fall in behind them before beginning their march.

A second line parade would follow the Mass. Based on the jazz funeral tradition, these parades invite anyone to join in - thus forming the "second line" behind the parade leaders and high-powered brass bands dressed in bright colors. Today's parade would dance in the streets down to Armstrong Park then over to the old U.S. Mint on Esplanade where the SummerFest stage was set up.

She searched for Sal and Bella, but couldn't spot them in the departing crowd. They must have been in the first wave to exit the church.

Echo nudged Moses, "Look who's here." As the church interior cleared, Echo noticed Teddy Stanton speaking with two men on the opposite side of the interior. "You and Hawke catch up with Maurice. I'll just go say a quick hello."

Across the center aisle she made her way between the pews lifting the kneelers with her foot. Curiosity darkened her eyes, "Good morning, Mr. Stanton. What a surprise seeing you here." She fanned the humid air around her face.

In a full suit and tie, Teddy appeared overdressed for the hot August interior of the church. He mopped his forehead with his ever present handkerchief.

Does this guy ever dress casually? she wondered.

Teddy Stanton didn't appear surprised to see her. "Hello, Victoria." Indicating the men to his right, he said "This is Brian Portman. He's a city councilman. And this is my business partner, Martin Silverman, who is also a councilman." He nodded to the petite blonde standing a way from Silverman speaking to someone else. "His wife, Alicia. The local politicians and businessmen like to show our support for this event since it's a notable one on our tourism calendar."

He placed his arm around Echo's shoulder, saying to his companions. "This is Esme Delahaye's granddaughter, Victoria LaBauve."

She controlled her shudder and used the excuse of shaking hands to move away from the over familiar gesture.

"Nice to meet you Mr. Portman. Mr. Silverman." Echo reached out and shook Martin's hand. FLASH! *Extreme Anxiety.* She recognized him as the passenger photographed with Nash the night before.

Silverman asked, "So I hear you're looking into those items found when Billy Williams' house was demolished. Have you discovered anything interesting?"

Echo considered Martin's eager posture and expression. *Were the found items the source of his anxiety?*

"We haven't uncovered anything yet." She flashed him a guileless smile, "Why? Do you know anything about the key, picture or cigarette case? Or why Billy would have hidden them?"

Silverman's eyes rounded in surprise at the questions she fired at him, looking quickly left to right from Stanton to Portman. He grinned and shrugged. "Me? I don't know anything. Just curious."

She touched Teddy's arm in a friendly gesture, pasted a smile on her face and backed away, "It was good to see you again Mr. Stanton, but I won't keep you. I need to rejoin my husband and friend."

FLASH! *Anticipation. Interference.*

The flashes were too ambiguous to make sense of but they triggered her radar. Maybe they were just two old guys fascinated with local mysteries.

Moses and Hawke sat in the folding chairs vacated by the musicians, talking quietly with the older black man. After introducing Echo when she joined them, Moses summarized what they had learned, "The piano player in the photo is Maurice's daddy. He died five years ago." His thumb hooked towards Maurice, Moses said "but he can give us a little second-hand history on Billy Williams."

His elbows resting on his knees, Maurice propped his chin on his hands, leaning forward. He contemplated where to start; squinting his large eyes with golden flecks.

He began, "Well my Daddy, Cap Jones, often played the same gigs with Billy. He spoke highly of him. Billy got a little famous and traveled, but my Daddy stayed local. They was Deacons together at this here church."

Echo pointed her hand fan to the picture Moses held. "Do you know any of the others in the picture?"

"I don't recognize anyone. My Daddy talked about a singer. Referred to her jokingly as Sister Mabel. Said she was much younger than them so they treated her like a sister." Tapping the picture, Maurice said, "I guess it could be her. But I don't know her real name. Nothing comes to mind about the guitar player."

Moses asked, "Do you have any ideas which club this photo was taken in or who the white man sitting at the table is?"

He smacked his lips and said, "Don't know anything about the white dude. Looks older than the others. Maybe a musician. Could also be the club manager or owner. A number of places on Bourbon Street have wooden panels like that. Fredericks. The Blues Bar. The Juice Club. The clubs have been around for ages; just keep changing names and owners."

Echo noted them in her tablet.

"The stories these joints could tell would probably curl your hair. The bands playing there were always local boys - white, black - it didn't matter - but they got together with one common goal - to play some good music and make a buck in the process."

Hawke quietly intervened, "What else can you tell us about Billy?"

Maurice shifted back in his chair, rubbing his bald head giving thought to Hawke's question. "He was different – for a black man. Daddy called him a champion. He spoke up for the musician rights."

"How so?"

"Aw man, all I can do is repeat stories I heard. The Jazz Clubs back then were linked to racketeering, graft, prostitution associated with a mob family. Musicians often had to pay a bribe or a percentage of their pay to get gigs at the most popular joints."

Maurice sighed, squirming in his seat. "According to Cap, Billy campaigned in his own way gainst the graft. No one made enough money with just music to support their families. You know what I mean?"

"Did your Daddy and Billy work together outside of music?" asked Echo.

"Nah" said Maurice. "My Daddy worked at the sugar mill. Billy worked as a finishing carpenter. Folks said he was as gifted with wood as he was with music. Cap said Billy made this little box for Sister Mabel using different kinds of wood fitted together like a jigsaw puzzle and polished to a high shine."

"Archer found a cigarette case and a key that he believes Billy hid." The computer tablet she held out to Maurice displayed a photo of each. Echo asked, "Do you have any idea what the significance of these items might be to Billy?"

"No idea. I doubt many black men carried silver cigarette cases back then." After a closer examination of the photo, he said "The key has a pretty head design and the millings appear to be hand-tooled. Somethin' an artisan would make."

Moses eyebrows twitched in thought. He commented, "That's a pretty specific observation. Are you an expert on keys or something?"

Maurice responded with an ironic bark of laughter. "I supplemented my income, working as a locksmith when I started out playing music. I got interested in old keys. They are pretty, but couldn't guard much. Many of them had the same generic grooves. Do you know one of them skeleton keys could open hundreds of locks?" His finger tapped the small key in the photo and he said, "That looks like a design custom fitted to a specific lock."

The rat-a-tat of a snare drum and tenor notes from a trombone drifted through the open doors.

"Thank you, Maurice. You've been helpful. I hope we didn't delay you from your marching club."

Horn in hand, Maurice gave them a bright smile and stood up. "No problem. They always mill around for awhile before beginning the march." He sauntered outside to join the other club members dressed in yellow suits.

From the open doorway, Echo, Moses and Hawke watched people fall in behind one of the three marching bands. The club members of each band dressed in coordinated suits and hats. Today's groups were garbed in yellow, pink and blue costumes. Their grand marshals blew whistles and waved feathered fans half the size of the man to lead the brass bands known as the first line. The brass band began propelling everyone's enthusiastic march through the street, blasting exuberant rhythms. Strutting, jumping and high-stepping underneath their decorated parasols and handkerchiefs the participants formed behind one of the parade bands – the second line parade.

Moses turned to Echo. "Who was the stout man with Stanton?"

"His partner, Martin Silverman, who I picked up a flash of anxiety from. Why do you ask?

"He looks like the guy who got out of the car Nash drove last night."

"He is. I recognized him from Zetta's snapshot. He asked about what we've discovered related to Archer's items, but claimed it was just curiosity." Echo shrugged and said, "Half the Quarter is curious and I'm dreaming about birds chasing hot potatoes."

"After we drop the car off in the parking garage, Echo and I are walking over to the stage at the Old Mint. The kids Poppy Rouge mentors for the Foundation are performing today. Want to join us?" asked Hawke

Moses shook his head, no. His lips formed a tight smile. "I think I'll pass. I'm with musicians most every night. I'll catch up with you tomorrow."

11

RIVERFRONT: *promenading*

Hawke parked his black SUV between Poppy's classic truck and Echo's metallic green Smart Car. Absent any driveways or garages for houses in their neighborhood on Royal, they kept reserved parking in a garage a couple of blocks from their home. Echo rarely used an automobile to get around the city and then only when she had multiple places to visit outside of the city center. A small, economical car suited her fine.

They exited the garage on Barracks Street and turned left. A floppy brim straw hat and oversize sunglasses to shield her face and shoulders from the blistering sun completed her ensemble of a black sleeveless blouse and straight leg pants, both made of cotton - the tailoring reminiscent of a nineteen fifties style. Hawke looked at her, holding her hand as they walked. He teased, "I feel like I'm strolling with a red headed Audrey Hepburn."

As they crossed Decatur Street, they spotted Poppy

shepherding five teenagers up the steps to the side of a stage. Tyrone, a music major at the University of New Orleans and the group's instructor, played drums for the band. The youngest, a thirteen year old girl sat at the piano running through finger exercises while she waited. Beryl was a high functioning autistic who played by ear. Although she could copy anything she heard perfectly, her autism kept her from extemporaneously playing riffs. The other band members had quickly adapted, scripting riffs for her to listen to and copy into their program. Big for his fourteen years, the members called the double bass player Fat Albert after the cartoon character – not due to his size - but because he was the heart of the group. Tall with broad shoulders, he towered over Poppy who was assisting him with moving the bulky bowed string instrument onto the stage. The last two members of the group, Jose and Miguel, were twin brothers playing cornet and sax.

Poppy couldn't play an instrument – or sing on key – but that didn't keep him from volunteering as counselor to this group of children who participated in the music program sponsored by the Foundation. He laughingly referred to himself as their spirit guide. The individuals had different stories and dissimilar backgrounds, but had formed a tight knit group. Because it was unlikely they would have become friends otherwise, they named their group the Unlikelies.

The Unlikelies had blossomed under Poppy's attention. He convinced Hawke and Moses to host an afternoon jazz tea at the Sunset Riff Club to give the ensemble an opportunity to play on stage before a live audience. An unexpected success, the Sunset Riff was planning to host similar teas once a quarter to showcase young musicians. Poppy then engineered a spot for the Unlikelies to perform on the SummerFest Stage.

The audience shushed. The first notes of music caught their attention. Plucking his bass, Big Albert began singing in an unusual gravelly voice for a fourteen year old... *Oh, the shark, babe, has such teeth, dear.* The crowd broke into a quick applause approving of the old standard "Mack the Knife".

Tyrone brushed his drums, adding a simple tempo with his symbols to kick off their next song "When You're Smiling". Poppy waved his arms to the crowd inviting them to sing along with the refrain *the whole world smiles with you.*

Hawke leaned in close to Echo's ear so she could hear him over the music, "There's Sal and Bella." He tipped his chin up to indicate the grass space on the far side of the stage.

A pouting young man stood with them. With accusing eyes staring from underneath a frown, he shook Sal's hand off his arm. Bella reached out saying something, but the male shook his head heatedly and trounced away.

"Who's the young guy?" Echo asked Hawke.

"I don't think I've ever seen him before."

"Hmmm," she murmured, remembering the flash of worry from Sal on Friday morning at Maurice's Museum Shop. Suspicion prickled. Echo wondered if Sal could be involved in Archer's mystery before turning her attention back to the stage.

Echo congratulated the Unlikelies on their performance when they finished their set. While they busied themselves putting away their instruments, she kissed Poppy on the cheek and said, "We'll see you back home tonight."

"Wait a minute. Fat Albert's grandmother wanted a word with you." Poppy waved over a black woman standing with the teenagers. Like her grandson, she was head and shoulders above Poppy. With an unlined face and straight posture, only the thin grey hair pinned in a tight bun hinted at her age.

Poppy introduced everyone. Encouraging the woman with his sparkling blue eyes and soothing voice, he said, "Amelia thought she might have some information related to your mystery."

"Miss Victoria," began Amelia "my grandson Albert is

72

always on the computer when he isn't practicing his music. He showed me a picture you put on that facebook thing," pursing her lips and arching her eyebrows to show she really didn't understand the internet social site.

"Well, anyway, I remember my Grand Ma'Ma talking about how she knew Billy Williams back in the day. She was younger than Billy, but sang in the choir so she knew of him from church. She used to tell about a girl who sometimes sang with Billy and his friends. Her name was Mabel." Amelia smile in reminiscence. "My Grand Ma'Ma had hoped someday to sing in clubs, but her Daddy wouldn't allow it."

Echo said, "Someone else today mentioned the girl in the photo could be named Mabel. Do you remember if your grandmother ever mentioned a last name?"

"Yes," replied Amelia. "She said her name was Mabel Ball. I only remember because Grand Ma'Ma used to laugh and say with a name like Ball, if she ever got famous she should change her name."

"Did your grandmother ever mention what became of Mabel?"

Shaking her head no, Amelia chuckled. "After Billy became famous, she probably remembered she met him in church. She told the same story snippets over and over."

Echo thanked Amelia and said goodbye again with a hug for Poppy. She tapped a message into her smart phone, sending Mabel Ball's name to Zetta and Moses to add to their research. "Well, now we know the names of three of the people in the mystery photo. Unfortunately, no one seems to know why that photo was important to Billy."

"I'm sure you'll figure it out, Sweetheart." Hawke tugged her towards the Riverwalk. "Come on, let's take a walk before heading home."

She couldn't resist ribbing him a little, "Are you sure you can handle promenading with a red-headed Audrey?"

Pulling her close to him, he ducked his head under the floppy brim of her hat. After a slow, thoughtful kiss, he murmured, "I'm proud to be with you anywhere."

She reached out lacing his fingers with her own. "I love you more than.." She always left the sentence open. Gently pulling him towards the Riverwalk, she tossed her head, "Let's promenade."

They leisurely followed the walkway along the riverside of the French Quarter, enjoying the breeze from the Mississippi - one of the world's busiest rivers.. Watching the traffic – cruise ships, tugboats, cargo ships and paddle wheelers – is enthralling to visitors and locals.

A saxophonist wailed a short, haunting tune to call the strolling tourists toward him. Hawke and Echo paused on their walk through Woldenburg Park to watch the musician. Garbed all in black, sunglasses and a beatnik cap, a battered horn case sat open at his feet, seeded with tip money. His wiry grey hair and beard spoke of his age. He played another quick scale to keep the interest of the building crowd then paused to roll his long sleeves to his elbows. A grandmother pushed a baby stroller up to his bench, sat and talked with the old guy while he oiled the keys on his horn, waiting for more people to join the crowd. Finally he wet his whistle and raised the horn to his lip. Smiling at the grandmother, he played "Braham's Lullaby". The old man responded to the surprise applause with a dip of his head and shifted into a rousing, fun tune to keep the crowd's interest.

Two benches farther, another street performer claimed his performance space along the walkway. His yellow painted grocery cart, decorated with Mardi Gras beads, ostrich feathers and a pink bra flying from a bamboo staff, also sported a multi-colored tire stretched around its frame as a bumper. The dark skinned, lanky boy arranged his instruments – a bongo drum, horn, Indian flute, maracas, tin can on the end of a stick – in and around his cart preparing to compete for attention and tips.

From this vantage point, it was obvious that the Mississippi really is above the level of the city. And you could see with your own eyes how New Orleans earned the nickname the Crescent City as the water vessels followed a dramatic turn in the river. Echo and Hawke meandered south until they reached the fountain in Spanish Plaza.

They bought Italian ice from one of the cart vendors then sat on a concrete seat in the large sunken space with beautiful inlaid tiles. Originally named Eads Plaza, the square was intended to memorialize the engineer who improved the navigation of the mouth of the Mississippi River. In 1976, Spain dedicated the Plaza to the City of New Orleans in remembrance of their common historical past. The plaza's focal point, a fountain surrounded by colorful seals of the provinces of Spain, synchronized to music and colors, created an enticing place to relax. Although the Plaza was a little tired looking, it offered a terrific view of the River.

Across the Plaza, two Macaws pranced along the frame of their owner's bicycle enchanting a group of children by mimicking them. Abraham and his large parrots were a common site in the Quarter. Scarlet and Indigo rode Abraham's bike everywhere with him. An old Vietnam vet who had functionally recovered from post traumatic stress disorder, Abraham lived in a boarding house of sorts somewhere in the city central, supplementing his disability pay by doing odd jobs for the local merchants and collecting tips from tourists with his social birds.

The red and yellow parrot danced on the handlebars, spun around, flared her wings and bowed to the children causing shrieks of laughter. The other parrot, Indigo, cocked his blue head staring out from eyes surrounded by black and white stripes and mocked the children's laughter. The children appeared content to stay and play with the birds for hours, but the parents, anxious to continue with whatever was on their tourist agendas, dropped tips into the straw hat on the ground next to the bike's front tire, gently pulling their youngsters away.

Abraham emptied the hat into his pockets. He looped the cord of the hat around his neck, arranged Indigo and Scarlet on his handlebars and walked away, upriver, his right hand grasping one handle to push the bicycle alongside him.

Echo finished her lemon ice, taking pleasure in the breeze off the river. This August Sunday was the last day of freedom before school for the teenagers and young parents milling in the plaza.

A screeching bird drew Echo's attention back to Abraham. He shrugged away from a man. The man moved closer to him, grabbing his arm. Abraham jerked back stumbling over his falling bike. Indigo flapped his wings, hopping up and down on the cocked handlebars. He squawked, "Stop!"

Scarlet joined in, mimicking Abraham. "Awwkk. You moron."

Hawke jumped up from the bench, running across the Plaza towards Abraham. Echo hurried after him, but her espadrille wedge shoes made it difficult to keep up.

Abraham rocked his shoulders side to side, continuously snapping his fingers and repeating, "No. No. No."

Echo tried to quiet him, "It's ok, Abraham. You're ok." She rested one hand on his arm, the other on his jumping knee, attempting to soothe him. *Flash..gun.. fury.. panic..leaden grey hue.*

Hawke searched for the man who had agitated Abraham, but he couldn't locate him in the crowd. Rejoining them, he said, "He probably disappeared into the Riverwalk Marketplace, mingling with shoppers." He stooped down to eye level with Abraham. "Do you know who that man was?"

"Anh, anh" Abraham said shaking his head no.

"Did he try to hurt you, Abraham?" Echo persisted.

Abraham sat on the ground petting his parrots to soothe them. He was still tense but less agitated. He looked down avoiding direct eye contact and mumbled, "Unknown."

Echo sat next to Abraham, absently rubbing her finger gently over Scarlet's head. She tried again to draw Abraham's focus.

Abraham breathed deeply, exhaling through his mouth. Ignoring Echo and speaking to his birds, he said softly, "He can't have you. Anh, Anh."

Obvious that they weren't going to get much more from Abraham after trying various questions, they just sat with him until he climbed on his bike with Scarlet and Indigo and rode away.

"Was it just me or was that a strange encounter?" Hawke reached down, grasping Echo's hand to help her to her feet.

"Yes. Pretty strange." Echo said. "I picked up an IF from Abraham. He believed the man had a gun. He had this instant of raging fury, then sudden panic and confusion. Now, it's my turn for strange. I only had a glimpse, but the man resembled that Nash guy from the club Friday night. You remember Mr. Cologne?"

Hawke guffawed, "What idiot would try to take Abraham's bird?"

Echo dusted the grass from her pants and said, "As Scarlet squawked, a moron."

♪♪

The loud, hoarse whistle of the calliope heralded the return of the steamboat *Natchez* from its river cruise. A blue harbor police boat idled in the river. One dark hand wrapped around her slender waist, Hawke stood close to Echo on the Riverwalk as the bright red paddle wheel ceased churning the muddy water. Passengers waited behind the white deck rails decorated in red, white and blue bunting while huge thrusters took over to maneuver one of the few stern wheelers remaining from the glory of the steamboat age sideways to its dock. Hawke and Echo basked in the warmth of the late afternoon sun midway on its path to the horizon, a companionable cocoon in the midst of exaggerated motions and activities typical of a tourist city during a festival weekend.

A complex woman, he knew her on so many levels of intimacy- in ways that alternately thrilled and frightened him. A person couldn't spend much time with Victoria without experiencing an intimate connection. Entranced by a nine year old titian haired girl, he fell in love with the twelve year old warrior princess. Her seductive power to involve others in her fight for the 'greater good' captured him on the school ground when she challenged a teenage bully to consider how the nerd he harassed might prove more beneficial as a friend than enemy. Recognizing the stubborn stance -hands planted on her hips, chin jutted out in determination, no fear- Hawke stepped up, standing mutely beside her. Moses followed his friend, joining them without uttering a word. And miraculously, other students stepped up forming a silent circle around the bully. Then Victoria disregarded the caution of others, sought out and befriended the bully, sensing something in him that others couldn't recognize. That bully, now a priest, credited Victoria's intuitive sense of inclusion for repairing his self-esteem.

The earlier tension was gone when Echo looked up at him, but something was flickering far back in her deep green eyes. So many levels of intimacy. Soul mates, best described by an Indian poem. *Strong as the eagle, soft as the dove, patient as the pine tree that stands in the sun and whispers to the wind...You are the One.* She was his one. Hawke trusted her senses, valued her intelligence and admired her courage yet her fearlessness and unpredictability often frightened him. Caging her spirit would destroy her yet thought of losing her weakened him.

Echo pressed her palm against his heart, catching her breath the jolt from fast, hard thumping.

Hawke covered her hand with his own, cradling it tightly against his chest. He exhaled a long sigh of contentment and assured her, "strong as the eagle." She understood.

In no hurry, they strolled, hand-in-hand toward Jackson Square, its four sides filled with locals, tourists, commerce and culture. Some artists removed their paintings from outside the iron fence, folded their camp chairs and stored their boxes of pastels and charcoals, packing up for the day. A few members of the open-air art colony hung around in a quest for late sales to straggling tourists.

Big Brush Charlie waved to them when they neared the Decatur Street entrance to the square. Eighty-nine years old and frail, Charlie was on the fence most Sundays during good weather, accompanied by a companion his family had insisted on for his safety. One of the foundation's first clients, he had insisted on paying for their help with one of his ethereal bayou scenes.

Charlie mixed his own paints. Every year he traveled the Gulf Coast, collecting clays from different regions to pigment his paints with a depth and radiance that couldn't be mimicked by chemical colorants. His large brush strokes layering earth colors achieved an early morning or evening glow in his swamp scenes, depending on how the light fell on the canvass.

"Hey, Echo," the old man called. "I want to talk to you about that old picture your girl posted on facebook."

"You do social networking, Charlie?" Echo seemed surprised.

"What? You think an old man ain't smart enough to

have online friends?"

His question flustered Echo, but before she could respond, Charlie said, "Don't worry. I'm just yanking your chain. One of my daughters bought me a computer when I was seventy. She set me up so I can stay connected with my great grandkids spread across the country – although I can't say that I have a need to know everything they post there." He rolled his eyes. "Some of these young kids think updating the world with their coffee choice is interesting news."

"Did you know anybody in the photo Zetta posted?" asked Hawke.

"Nope. But I have an observation for you. You know, back around the time that picture was taken, I did charcoal sketches on Bourbon Street. That was before I painted in oil."

"So you recognize the place?" Echo asked, eager to get to the point.

"Nooo," Charlie drawled, subtly reminding her to be patient. "It's about the man's suit. I had to think about it before I could figure out what bugged me. I think you should look at mob connections."

Hawke squeezed Echo's hand to still her fidgeting, cautioning her not to interrupt yet.

Charlie rubbed his chin, satisfied with his conclusion. "That's a gangsta suit. Back then, gangsters afforded the new styles before the average Joe. It wasn't until the end of the war and rationing that businessmen had new tailored suits and then they copied the gangster style."

His thin lips parted in a smile at a kindled memory. "Even then I couldn't afford it, and you could say that I really coveted that look."

"I'm no expert on historical styles, but couldn't a wealthy businessman have owned a new suit earlier than most other people?"

The old man frowned. "Yeah, that's possible. Those

black and white wingtips he's wearing were also copied into fashion after the war. But what convinced me the man in your picture really was a gangster is his fedora. Back then you could tell a gangster from a businessman by the way they snapped the front brim of their hat."

Echo hugged his thin shoulders, "Charlie, you certainly have given me an unusual clue to follow. Thanks for your perception."

Charlie grinned, tapping the tip of his nose with his forefinger. "I may not have the insight that comes with your streak of white hair, but I like to believe as an artist I've been bestowed with a keen observation."

The thin peal of the St. Louis Cathedral bells rang slightly off-key calling the time- a quarter to five from the far side of the square as they meandered along the circular walkway. The oldest Catholic cathedral in the entire United States was established as a parish in 1720 which explains why Louisiana has parishes instead of counties like other states have. Inside the cathedral basilica, flags mounted high overhead the pews represent the countries once dominant in New Orleans. The church with its three turquoise spires stood sentinel to a plaza - home to street performers, artists, and palm and tarot card readers - neither judging nor joining.

A petite woman rose from a chair splattered with dozens of paint colors when they exited the gate framed by black iron pillars topped with gas lanterns. From this prime location she could snag the tourists immediately upon their exit from the pristine square to the circus atmosphere of the plaza which fronted the cathedral. Large sequins with tiny bells tinkled on the edges of a headscarf wrapped around her black hair and the pointed boots beneath the flounce of her skirt completed her gypsy costume.

"Saw your grandfather last night on Julia Street. Found myself a bench, too, and took advantage of the foot traffic."

Pauline flashed a sly grin of amusement, "That sure is a pretty picture of you two in the paper today."

As Zetta had predicted, the newspaper leaned toward a Mr. and Mrs. Elegant caption for their photo. Echo struggled with an internal conflict. *How could she feel comfortable in the moment, but later feel that pictures of herself on the society pages screamed pretender?*

"Maybe because they portray only a superficial view." Pauline said reading her unstated thoughts. "You're not a fraud. You're complex. Your friends understand you as you are." She clapped her hands then swished them back and forth across each other in a washing motion as if to rid the air of Echo's conflicting emotion.

Hawke agreed with Pauline.

Skirts swished and bells jingled as Pauline stood on one high heel boot, using her other foot to turn herself left in a circle three times. She placed her right hand on Hawke's chest over his heart and stared fixedly into his deep brown eyes.

"Beware of the smelly man, but don't fret. You'll be close enough."

12

ROYAL STREET: *colligating*

He closed the grill lid, catching Poppy's attention through the residual smoke. He kept his voice low, his eyes shifting to Echo across the lawn. "She's been quiet and preoccupied in thought since the incident with Abraham earlier today. I know she can handle herself in tough situations, but I can't help worrying about her safety since she had the flash about a gun."

"She sensed a leaden grey color. What does that signify?" asked Hawke.

"Meanness." Poppy delivered his matter-of-fact response with a solemn expression.

Glancing to confirm Echo wasn't listening, Hawke said, "I'll ask Moses to stay closer to her over the next couple of days. And let's you and I find reasons to join her during the day. I'm free until next week."

Poppy spoke softly, "We can try, but our Echo is pretty stubborn about her independence. She's not going to take kindly to us hovering."

Clad in cut-off shorts and a faded National Geographic t-shirt, her bare feet moved on the moss stones as Echo slowly and repetitively sequenced through her Tai Chi movements. She had discovered the solo form of Tai Chi in college, enabling her to stimulate and clear blocked pathways in her mind. The meditative movements heightened her cognition, allowing her to dig deeper into her intuitive thoughts, assemble order and hierarchy or simply reason through many pieces of what appeared unrelated information.

A harrowing experience while chasing a story during her investigative reporter days had prompted Echo to expand her training in Tai Chi to include the fundamental principles of martial art. Her instructor, Ms. Shu, taught her to incorporate her learned movements into an assortment of attacks and defenses. Since then, to the dismay of her Grandmother, she had used the martial art form on several occasions to defend herself. So she maintained her skill, sometimes practicing with Moses. Esme worried that it gave her a false sense of safety, calling it foolish fearlessness.

One more contentious subject between them, her martial arts practice contradicted the persona Esme attributed to a lady. Her grandmother considered this just another dichotomy to be corrected. In her mind, there was a simple solution. "Stop this ridiculous mystery work and you wouldn't need to know martial arts."

As fearless as Echo was with every other aspect of her life, she dodged outright confrontation with the grandmother who had become her mother. She convinced herself that evasion was the best pathway to family harmony. Her parents died in a car crash when she was nine. Grandmother Esme and Poppy Rouge –after much discussion and some drama— decided she would live with Poppy until they could discover what special abilities Echo would inherit from her Leger ancesters. Rouge, her mother's father, packed Echo's belongings into his 1962 Ford truck and drove her across the Atchafalaya Basin to his cottage in Breaux Bridge.

Although loved by both grandparents, their parenting techniques had been poles –and societies- apart. By age eleven, she had decoded their approaches, adapting her behavior and style based on environment and circumstances. She remembered a few colossal clashes with her grandmother during the time she struggled to identify herself.

In addition to the typical traumatic moments many teenagers experienced, she sometimes suffered isolation because other teens couldn't understand her idiosyncratic abilities. Grandmother Esme chose to ignore the elephant in the room – that Echo was different – or to accept those differences as a talent or gift. There simply was no etiquette defined for how to socialize her special abilities. Poppy Rouge helped her embrace her paradoxes. She had established some autonomy during her university years through trial and error, slowly managing to integrate her unique talents with social skills.

Tonight she practiced the meditative form, allowing her thoughts to flow in random patterns, considering facts, people and intuitive moments linked to Archer's discovery of the photo, cigarette case and key.

The slap of a screen door infringed on Echo's meditation. She transitioned from the *Flying Dove Spreads its Wings* movement into a closing posture. Imagining she was scooping water in her hands to cool her forehead, she used the sides of her palms to brush away any spills down the front of her body. Breathe in slowly. Breathe out slowly. Breathe in. Breathe out. She squinted into the hues of muted gold falling below the fence line - hands planted on her hips, lips pursed in reflection, head cocked to one side. The sun slowly closed the curtain on Sunday -.

Poppy watched his granddaughter and couldn't help

remembering a nine year old Victoria with her bare feet planted in the soft grass at the bayou side declaring who she was going to be when she grew up. Five feet seven inches tall, his skin burned dark from years of working his orange grove in the sun, the humor lines around his blue eyes added kindness and ease to his face. His neat plaited red tail fell well below his shoulders. He whistled to get her attention and held up a bottle of wine.

"Why don't you have a glass while Hawke grills our dinner and tell us what you're colligating, Shă?"

Freeing her hair from the scrunchie, Echo shook out her curls and joined them on the patio. She accepted the red wine from her grandfather and plopped into a chair. Her hair, exploding from the humidity, appeared cinnamon in the falling light.

She sipped her wine, giving Hawke and Poppy a serene smile.

"Mostly, I've been ordering information pieces, people and intuitive flashes – mulling over their possible relationships. More importantly, the gaps of knowledge. It's been so long since that photo was taken that the people we talked with know of Billy Williams and Cap Jones and Mabel Ball but they don't *know* them. Someone –who identity is unknown– has something to protect and no one recognizes what or why." Remembering Big Brush Charlie's perceptions, she asked, "And what would gangsters have to do with this?"

Undaunted, she looked up from under her long lashes after another taste of her wine and declared, "Tomorrow I start digging further to uncover the underlying story because I'm convinced there is one."

Poppy cautioned, "Just be extra aware. Your digging could wake a nest of rattlers."

"Isn't it Moses' role to protect me from rattlers?" Echo cunningly referred to Hawke's stipulation she retain Moses when she formed the Foundation. She had bristled at his insistence, often making it difficult for Moses in the initial days of the Foundation. Now, most days, she acknowledged it was a smart decision.

Poppy's blue eyes sparked with amusement. "Sassy thing, you are. Just remember rattlers rarely bite unless they are provoked or threatened. Pay attention. Best course of action if you hear a rattle, is to back away before the snake can strike."

After Echo and Hawke cleaned up the remnants of their grilled salmon and asparagus dinner they wished Poppy goodnight. While Hawke locked the doors and set the alarm system, Echo climbed the circular staircase, undressing along the way. He followed her trail of clothing into their bedroom, drawing her to him.

"I need to feel you close to me tonight," he whispered pressing his face to her hair. She heard him draw a breath, long and quiet, releasing it. His arms tightened around her. The smoldering flame she saw in his eyes struck a vibrant chord in her.

With a sense of urgency and intense passion, they danced the erotic ballet of lovers.

♫♪

The fluttering overhead pulled her eyes up towards the sky. Instead of using his wings, the man bird parachuted down under an umbrella. Gripping its handle, shaped liked a pistol; he maneuvered the large parasol to land on her shoulder. He wore galoshes instead of wheels for feet. No sooner he perched, he pecked her.

"Ouch. Why did you do that?" she asked, rubbing the crown of her head.

"Hurry up, Girl. I'm tired of waiting," gooney man bird said, worrying his wings over her face before hopping to the ground. When she opened her eyes, his galoshes were gone and the wheels back in

place. He tossed the umbrella down, lit a cigarette and whizzed away.

A cool breeze across her bare shoulders stirred her awake. She shifted closer to the strength and warmth of Hawke's sleeping body next to her.

The soft sway of the dream catcher Hawke had given her long ago - now an ornament attached to the ceiling fan chain - lulled her back into a restless sleep.

13

ROYAL STREET: *chaperoned*

The aroma of coffee and voices floating up the stairs nudged her from sleep. The chill of the air conditioning on her naked body brought her fully awake. Quickly moving to her closet, she dressed for comfort in navy pants and pastel t-shirt. After lacing up her tennis shoes, she grabbed a cap and moved her tablet, phone and lip gloss to a cloth bag. *Ok, Monday. Here I come.* An urgent need to discover something meaningful drove her downstairs towards the voices at the rear of the house.

She skipped down the stairs. Rounding the curved banister, she called out to the two most important men in her life, "Morning, Poppy. Morning, Hubby."

"Good morning Shă," answered Poppy from his perch on a stool next to the wide granite counter.

Damp hair tied back in a short pony tail; Hawke lounged in runner's shorts against the kitchen island a steaming coffee mug cradled in his hands.

Echo popped a blueberry bagel into the toaster and slid an herbal tea packet into the brewer near Hawke. She patted his derriere running her eyes in an exaggerated slow perusal of his long, dark legs. "Aren't you the early bird, fitting in a morning jog before I'm awake?"

"You mean before the humidity smothers me."

Hawke grabbed her by the waist pulling her close, his liquid caramel eyes questioning. "Where are you hurrying off to already?"

Slathering cream cheese on her bagel, she said "Archer left a message on my phone that he found some old stuff of Billy's in the attic. I plan to pick those up. And I hoped to poke around the Jazz Preservation Hall. Not sure what information they have, but.."

Hawke placed his finger under her chin, tipping her face up to his, interrupting her. "You have shadows under your eyes. Rough dream night?"

Not wanting to worry him further by mentioning the gun, she made light of the dream. "Oh, you know. Another one of Alice's rabbit holes. I just wish I was a better prognostic."

Poppy teased her, "Yeah. You're an embarrassment to the Legers."

"You do remember you instruct an etiquette session today, don't you?" asked Hawke.

Echo sighed noisily, rolling her eyes. "I haven't forgotten. I can do a quick change at the office and still make it there in time."

"Mind if I walk with you to the Foundation this morning? I have a couple of healing appointments later, but I thought I'd check in earlier with Corinne - take inventory of her stock of my specialty teas." Poppy created his own brand of blended teas from a workshop in his converted half of the outbuilding that also housed Hawke's working studio.

She pointed at Poppy, "You're welcome to walk with me

if you don't mind the stops I make along the way. Meet you out front."

"I'll drive you to the school since I promised Esme I would do head shots for her diplomat protocol class." Hawke said nonchalantly. He rinsed his coffee mug and placed it in the sink.

Eyes alert, her mouth turned up into a corner smile, she asked cheekily, "And is someone going to babysit me on my walk home today, too?"

"Ok, Miss Smarty-pants," he laughed. "Just trying to make sure Pauline's prediction that I'm close enough is true." He kissed her ear and asked, "What about you wait for me at the Foundation when your day ends? We can grab a meal then stop at the Riff on our way back."

Save the argument for a more important occasion. If he knew she dreamed about a gun-handled umbrella, he'd demand more than Poppy as an escort. Echo hugged him back and agreed. "Dinner. It's a date." She hung her bag off her shoulder and headed to the front door. "I'd better not keep my first chaperone waiting."

Warm, still air washed over her when she stepped outside. She found Poppy patiently sitting on the stoop checking items in a satchel. The bag stirred memories of happy, innocent days on the bayou. Wanting to give her grandfather something special on Father's Day, Echo had asked Hawke's mother for help. She cut and sewed a sack that Poppy's tea leaf shipments arrived in, transforming it into a tote bag with pockets. Twelve years later, Poppy still wore the burlap satchel to carry his healing potions and tea mixtures.

Echo pulled on a plaid newsboy cap, shading her face from the early morning sun. She climbed down the steps, edging around him, tapped his head and asked "Ready?"

As they headed out, Poppy called to Miss Margie on her balcony, "anything exciting happening?"

Margie primped and gave a finger wiggle wave. She

was in full makeup this morning, her lips a slash of scarlet red to match her painted fingernails. "Mornin' Rouge. Echo. The street's quiet yet this morning."

♪♪

Two thin leather straps dangled from the handlebars of the rusty blue bicycle propped against the wall under the front window of Sal's Market. "Interesting. That looks like Abraham's bike. Wonder what he's doing here?" Echo commented to her grandfather before they entered the store.

Huddled, with their heads together over something laid on the counter, Bella and Sal looked up at the sound of the bell jangling on the door. Poppy sauntered to the scrabble game where a young man with tattoos and a Mohawk contemplated the board and a rack of tiles while he sipped a coffee. Five vowels and two consonants, y and n. The only open consonant was a g. Together they mulled over different play options.

Echo selected today's newspaper from the stand inside the front door moving straight ahead to the register counter.

"Is that Abra...?"

"Did you see..?"

Bella and Echo started speaking at the same time. Echo paused and indicated Bella should continue.

Bella tapped her finger down on the open newspaper in front of her. "Since you're getting the paper just now, you probably haven't seen this yet. Check the metro section. The article about treasure hunters. What a hoot! Some blogger got people stirred up. They dug up holes all over Billy Williams' property before the neighbors reported them and the police chased 'em away."

Sal harrumphed. "Fools. Now Archer has to fill the holes to make sure no one gets hurt on the lot and tries to sue him. Inheriting that property has been nothing but a headache for the kid."

"Looks like Billy's treasure has gone viral," Echo said. Their puzzled expressions made it plain her attempt at humor fell flat so she explained. "With the internet, news travels fast, whether it's true or not. One person passes it on to others and they pass it on – and it's not long before an urban legend is born." She shrugged her shoulders to indicate you can't do much about the irrational behavior resulting from the blogger's hype.

"Is that Abraham's bike outside?" asked Echo, tipping her head toward the shop's front window.

"Yeah," said Sal. He pointed his thumb toward the back supply room of the shop. "He's working for the next couple of days for me, Archer and the art store down the street. Every few months a recycle truck comes through. Abraham takes care of breaking down the boxes and stacking the cardboard. We pay him a day rate and we let him keep the money he gets from the recycler."

"Where are his birds?"

Bella responded, "Oh, he brings them back there with him. They stay near him. Don't fly away."

"How was Abraham this morning? Did he seem upset or anything?" asked Echo.

Sal frowned, giving the question some thought. "Nah. Just sullen like he can be sometimes when he's not interested in talking. Why do you ask?"

Echo pulled her tablet from her bag, tapped an icon then slid her finger over the screen flipping through photographs until she found the picture Moses had snapped of Larry Nash on White Linen night. She showed the photo to Sal. "I think this man may have upset him yesterday. Have you seen this guy?"

Sal spoke around the unlit cigar clamped between his teeth, "No. Who is he?"

Up on tiptoes, Bella peeked over his shoulder at the

photo. "Yes, Sal. He was here last week."

Sal twisted his neck to look back at Bella. He sounded cranky, "How are you so sure? We get a lot of people through here every day."

"I remember telling you he wasn't local. Yet he didn't seem like a tourist so I wondered how he found his way into our store. He was dressed all in black – long sleeves, jeans and pointed boots made out of some kind of skin - in the hottest month in New Orleans. Posturing is what my Mama would have called it. At the time, I thought 'he's an out-of-town hood'."

Hood. How germane was Charlie's gangster observation?

"Did he ask you any questions? What was he doing while he was here?"

Bella bit her bottom lip, thinking. "He was here on Friday after Archer's store was broken into. He bought a sandwich - which he didn't eat. Don't think he ever ate a muffaletta before."

The Muffuletta is an Italian sandwich created in the late 1800's. The sandwich originated when Italian merchants working in the markets of New Orleans placed a mixture of broken green and black olives, found on the bottom of olive barrels, on a loaf of round Italian bread known as "muffs." Over this mixture, they layered slices of ham, salami and Provolone cheese.

"He just kind of hung around the scrabble board. Now that I think back on it, maybe he was mostly interested in listening in on all the talk about Archer and his Uncle Billy."

From across the shop they heard, "Whoop! Yeah, Dude." The young man plunked the tiles on the board and called out. "y-o-u-n-g. Forty-five points." He reached over with his fist, giving a pretend punch to Poppy's arm saying, "Catch you later."

After the young man left, Poppy flipped the game token

and crossed the room to join them at the counter.

Sal pointed his cigar at Echo. "What about you? Have you discovered anything related to those items Archer found? That fancy cigarette case. Or come up with any better ideas than that blogger what the key belongs to?"

"Not much." Still harboring a slight suspicion of Sal, she said with reticence, "I know a few names of the people in the photo, but no real clues yet about the items. I'm on my way to Archer's now."

As she turned to leave, Poppy asked Bella, "How are things going with your cousin's son?"

Bella and Sal glanced at each other, then back to Poppy. Bella sighed. "Yesterday afternoon he walked away angry after we tried reasoning with him. I'm not sure he will let us help him. I don't know what time he finally came home last night, but he was sleeping in his room this morning when we left."

With soothing blue eyes looking out from his weathered face, he gentled their anxiety, "I'll stop by again. Sometimes it's easier to open up to a stranger. Maybe he'll talk with me."

Echo didn't have to ask the question. Before they entered the next door to Archer's store, Poppy explained about the nineteen year old cousin. His mother and sister were killed in a car accident in Alabama when the driver of an eighteen wheeler had fallen asleep at the wheel. The cousin had been driving the car but survived. With no other close relatives, Bella and Sal had invited him to stay with them for a while. They were hoping he would transfer to a local university for the Fall semester to be near family. It is a sad situation, but maybe Poppy could help him heal.

"Whew," Echo said, exhaling noisily. "I'm ashamed to admit that my imagination had taken flight." She ticked facts off on her fingers. Sal has an intense interest in Archer's mystery. This weekend I kept bumping into him. He and Bella attended the Jazz Mass, but it felt like Sal was avoiding me.

Later near the stage, they had a heated discussion with a stranger. And this morning, Sal denying he ever saw Larry Nash."

With a sigh of relief, she said, "I guess I can move Sal lower on my suspect list for being involved in the break-in at Archer's store. He was probably distracted by the cousin situation."

"But I am leery about the coincidence of Abraham working for Archer on the day after he's approached by a stranger with a gun."

♫♫

Fifteen feet further, they entered Archer's Museum Store. Wiping his dusty hands on a cloth, his lanky body dressed in wide leg jeans and a t-shirt emblazoned with a peace sign, Archer ambled from the store room doorway towards them.

Phfeet. Phfeet. The loud whistle was followed by "Where you going boy?"

His eyes crinkling in laughter, Archer yelled back, "I'll be back Indigo. Hold your horses."

"Awwwkk. Hold your horses. Hold your horses. Awwkk," mimicked the McCaw.

"Sounds like you have company," said Poppy.

Archer shrugged his dreads back. "Abraham is in the backroom breaking down boxes. It's a package deal, you know. Him and his birds, but they can be fun."

He brought out a large paper shopping bag from under the counter. "Here are the shoe boxes I found in the attic. Only a few of the pictures have people's names written on the back and Billy kept some old programs and clippings. I skimmed through the contents but didn't notice anything that's an obvious connection to the silver case or key."

Elbows propped on the glass counter top, he rested his chin in his hands. "Well, I still don't know if I believe there's a real mystery, but that blogger guy sure has people running around the city looking for a rainbow of gold."

Poppy chuckled. "Sal told us they dug up holes in your lot."

"Not only that," his deep set eyes sympathetic. "St. Augustine had to hire security guards. They caught people searching for secret panels in the church. They invaded the church's out building taking down the wooden crosses and digging through boxes. No respect!"

"Have anyone contacted you again about the key?" Echo asked Archer.

"Nothing since that first day. I never responded to their texts and they never called." Archer's eyes slid back to Echo. "Have you found anything?"

Echo picked up the plastic frame with the photograph of the five people. She pointed to the piano player. "This is Cap Jones. I met his son, Maurice, playing horn at St. Augustine's Jazz Mass. Cap is no longer alive. Maurice didn't know what the significance of the cigarette case or key could be."

"Your uncle was a Deacon at St. Augustine. Maurice mentioned Billy worked as a finishing carpenter and was as gifted at that as music. Those facts are probably why people are searching for hiding places in the church. He remarked about the key's uniqueness which we plan to follow up on. Do you remember your Daddy or Uncle ever mentioning a key or secret?"

Archer cocked his head back and closed his eyes in thought. He puckered and smacked his lips. With an apologetic look for not being more helpful, he said, "I'm sorry, Echo. I just don't remember them ever talking about anything like that in front of me. No special key or lock, no secrets. Nothing more than regular, everyday stuff."

Disappointed, Echo pointed to the woman in the picture. "We believe this is a blues singer named Mabel Ball." She asked Archer, "Ever hear of her?"

He slapped his forehead. "I almost forgot," said Archer handing Echo a piece of paper. "I got this from a couple of old-timers."

Echo read the names hand written on the back of an old coupon advertisement. "Sister Mabel. We'll start tracing her today. Jerry Melancon. Mitchel Bourque." Her bright eyes looked up from under the brim of her cap. "Who are they?"

Archer pointed to the guitar player in the photo. "Those are names of two people who often played strings with Billy back when he first started. These old-timers aren't old enough to have known Uncle Billy personally. They didn't actually recognize anyone. They just know of names." He glanced apologetically at Poppy who was probably older than the guys he referred to as 'old-timers'.

"Ok," said Echo. "We'll try tracing these two names, too."

"Oh," Archer said with a sheepish grin. "Both of those people are no longer living, either. And the old ti-. Uhmm, I mean the guys didn't know if they had any family still alive."

His cobalt blue eyes twinkling, Poppy touched Archer's arm and said, "Don't worry son. I don't mind being called old. I think W. Somerset Maugham summed it beautifully. *The beauty of the morning and the radiance of noon are good, but it would be a very silly person who drew the curtains and turned on the light in order to shut out the tranquility of the evening.*

Before Archer could work through the meaning of the quote, Poppy concluded for him. "Old age has its pleasures. Although different, they are not necessarily less than the pleasures of youth."

Echo lifted the bag of photos. "I'll stay in touch, Archer." She cautioned him as they exited the store. "Be sure to call me if anyone approaches you again about the key."

"Well, *old-timer*, are you up to one more stop before we shuffle on to the office?" Echo teased Poppy. Turning serious, she said, "Let's detour to Bourbon Street. I'm curious about what the Jazz Preservation Hall has stashed in the way of information."

"Anywhere with you, Shă."

14

Downtown: *clash*

"What were you thinking, hiring him?" he asked with a horrified expression of disapproval. "Can you imagine my embarrassment when I heard Nash is linked to a mid level Mafia hoodlum?"

His partner showed total unconcern. "Where did you hear that?"

"I don't remember. Nash drove us to an event. Someone saw him and commented. The fact that you've been seen more frequently socializing with Candela from the DioGuardi family lends some credence to the comment. What's that all about anyway?"

The partner exhaled, blowing smoke and simply shrugged.

He twitched his nose, waving his hand in front of his face as he paced, "You need to quit smoking those cigars in here. It reeks."

"And you need to stop acting like a little old lady worrywart," the partner said from his plush leather chair, waving his cigar with disdain.

He stopped pacing when the door swung open.

"You wanted to see me, Mr. S?"

Both businessmen glowered at the driver, stopping him short. Nash backed out of the door. "Sorry for the interruption. I'll just wait out here until you two are done."

Exasperated, he raised his voice for the first time. "I'm not as blasé as you about how this can affect my character. I inherited more than wealth. My family reputation was built by hard work and integrity and I intend to maintain it."

"You're not the only one with a familial honor to protect," his partner warned from his chair, heavily exhaling cigar smoke. The partner's eyes hardened, measuring his colleague's reaction.

The taller partner abruptly turned on his heel and stalked back to his own office, past the *Flower in the Raindrop* photo displayed on the reception wall. He slammed his door shut.

♪♪

He slumped against the door and relaxed a fraction before dialing the phone. "I don't know if I rattled him enough to attempt a private meeting with the DioGuardi family."

Ending his call, he leaned his heavy body, planting his ear to the door frame, keeping vigil until he detected Nash's footsteps retreating through the lobby.

15

The Foundation: *echo girl*

They turned into the courtyard of the Foundation. Poppy waved to Corinne. "Catch up with you later," he said to Echo, heading towards the tall, statuesque black lady with short cropped hair who commanded their attention.

At their first meeting, Corinne had dealt with Poppy like a hedgehog with its quills extended. Echo remembered when she introduced Poppy as a healer, Corinne crossed her arms, arched her eyebrows in cynicism and simply said, "Unh huh," which Echo thought odd coming from someone who claimed to read tea leaves.

With a few long strides, Corinne met Poppy by the fountain, grasped his hand and pulled him towards one of the umbrella-shaded tables. She glanced back, her eyes glinted with humor, and called to Echo, "Rumor is you have strangers searching for treasure. Can't wait to hear more about that story."

Echo rolled her eyes and chuckled, continuing across

the cobblestones to the office.

She dropped Archer's tote bag containing the shoe boxes onto the floor, sank into the couch and jumped right into the middle of whatever Zetta and Moses had been doing. "I've got an hour before I need to change and leave. Can we do a quick recap of what we've discovered?"

Moses pulled his head out of the refrigerator and pointed to Zetta. "First, girl genius will give us a tutorial on the additional security she installed."

From her gaming chair, Zetta tapped her keyboard, blanking out all images on the wall screen. "It's simple. I reprogrammed the sequences. When you key in the code prior to swiping your hand on the exterior plate, the system assumes you are leaving and initiates a motion sensor web cam recording."

Zetta pointed her remote and a video of Zetta and Echo, captured during the brief minutes of the blackout, played onscreen. "Moses doesn't appear because the camera range is limited. The hundred twenty degree angle covers our entrance, base of the stairs and center work space."

"That takes care of leaving the building," she said. "Upon entering, the code after your hand scan deactivates the alarm as always. But the security cam keeps recording until you switch it off – which you do with the remote."

"Ok, now back to business." She pointed her remote and a photo of Larry Nash dominated the flat screen. "He's a nobody."

A few more documents joined Nash's image onscreen. "Couldn't find an address in New Orleans. His last driver's license shows an address in Norco. No current phone listing and the utilities linked to the driver's license address are under the name of Phyllis Nash. Maybe a wife or mother? Nothing on the parish property records."

Moses picked up the recitation, "No employment

appears on the tax rolls for the last two years. One arrest in St. Charles Parish for assault, but the charges were dropped. And we couldn't find a gun permit in his name."

Echo huffed, her eyes sparking, "I'm sure he was the guy who troubled Abraham yesterday. He definitely has weasel vibes. I don't believe it's a coincidence that I never saw him before, and then he appears in our world a couple of times in the same weekend."

She sat up from her slouch, pointing her finger in Moses' direction, "Oh, and Bella said he was hanging around their store Friday afternoon, showing interest in the local talk about Archer. So is he a dead end?" she asked.

"Not yet," Moses said. "I'm going to take a little road trip to Norco today. At least check out his listed address. And I'll be making a stop along the way. We think we've located Sister Mabel's granddaughter."

"That's good news." Echo looked at Zetta and asked, "Where is she?"

Pushing her glittery, chartreuse glasses back into position on her nose, Zetta explained. "Well, I was able to trace her through vital statistics records. It appears Mabel's daughter is deceased, but she has a granddaughter, Violet Boudreaux, who lives on Carrollton Avenue. I lost Mabel's trail after a second marriage."

Excited, Echo said, "Great. I want to meet her."

"Yeah, well, we tried calling her home but no one answered," said Moses. "So I thought I would swing by there before driving out to Norco and confirm her relation to Mabel. Then I'll arrange a time for you to meet."

Tossing his empty water bottle into the recycle bin, he walked out of the kitchen and settled into the opposite end of the couch from Echo. He rested his size eleven boots on the cypress table, leaned back lacing his hands together behind his head, and in his smooth bass voice said, "And one more thing. I had Zetta do a background check on Maurice Jones and scan for stories mentioning Cap Jones. No red flags. Both seem to be nice, ordinary folk. Nothing suggests Maurice had a reason to break into Archer's store searching for the key."

"Now, what goodies did you bring to us?" Zetta indicated the bag at Echo's feet.

"Archer located some photos and clippings that belonged to his great uncle. You and I can look through them this afternoon after my session at Esme's," said Echo.

"A couple of old guys gave this to Archer." She handed the scrap of paper to Zetta. "Names of musicians who played with Billy. Can you find something on these names or link them to the guitar player in the newspaper photo? I also stopped at the Jazz Preservation Hall this morning. Volunteers man their unofficial archive. They suggested I go back tomorrow when someone more knowledgeable would be available to help me." Turning to Zetta, she asked, "Want to meet me in the morning to archive dive?"

Zetta squeezed her eyes shut as if in pain. "I don't suppose those archives are computerized?"

With a snorted laugh her grandmother would not have approved of, Echo replied, "My guess is paper."

At the sound of cymbals crashing, all three turned to face the wall screen. One of Zetta's animated alarms, a marching cartoon drum major, reminded them of a calendar event.

Moses stood, "Time for me to drive."

Echo extended her hand for Moses to assist her up and off the couch. "I need to change clothes. Hawke will be here in a few minutes."

The back corner of the office contained an armoire and a full bathroom. Thankfully, she had just enough time for a quick shower.

♫♪

She twisted her hair into a loose chignon, assessing her reflection in the mirror on the wardrobe door. An oversized tiger eye teardrop necklace completed her ensemble of brown pencil skirt, beige silk blouse and low pumps. *Simple but enough to transform her to the professional persona expected by Grandmother Esme.*

Zetta sauntered up behind her, musing aloud, "You know, that corner is your equivalent of Superman's phone booth." She sang, "It's a Mystery Sleuth, it's a Socialite. No, it's just Echo Girl."

"Assisted by her sidekick, Zetta, the girl with the capacity to crunch virtual data as good as any top NASA analyst!" shot back Echo her eyes crinkled in humor.

"But, girl, your intuition works faster than a super CPU." Zetta pursed her lips in a pout, "It's just too bad you can't flash on demand."

Echo remembered the Dr. Seuss line Hawke quoted last night, "It's not about what it is, it's about what it can become."

Before walking out to meet Hawke, she instructed Zetta. "In addition to researching those musician names, will you investigate the source of that newspaper article about the blogger and Billy's treasure?"

"On it, Boss."

16

Carrollton and Norco: *moses involved*

Live oaks lining the wide avenue created an open air arch over the traffic moving in concert with the signal lights - sometimes ahead, sometimes behind- the streetcar rolling on tracks down the median. The Carrollton neighborhood, formerly a separate town, was annexed by the city of New Orleans in the late 1800's, although the post office still delivered mail addressed to Carrollton, Louisiana. Most of Carrollton had long been ethnically mixed where free people of color had owned homes and many immigrants settled into the neighborhood.

Moses found the address he searched for at the point where the pavement narrowed to one lane. After parking his Jeep in an open spot on the side street, he walked back round the corner to the clapboard residence which stood between a coffee house and a double shotgun house. This part of Carrollton is documented as the location of Rising Sun Hall near the riverfront in the late nineteenth century, reportedly owned by a Social Aid & Pleasure Club. Old storytellers claim the place, rented out for dances and functions, was the inspiration for the legendary song, "House of the Rising Sun".

A few paces after he opened the short wrought iron gate, he climbed three concrete steps onto the stoop of a house, its rose painted exterior accentuated with a dark grey front door. Mismatched rockers sat on the porch suggesting the occupants spent some of their time people watching. A low buzz of voices drifted from the left side property where patrons sunned outside at tables nursing their lattes, cappuccinos or iced coffees, playing with their phones and laptops. *Everyone was connected nowadays* thought Moses.

No one answered his knock. He peeped through the glass partially covered by a lace curtain and knocked again, harder. Still no response. He wrote a brief message on a Foundation business card asking Violet to call and lodged it between the frame and door near the handle hoping the owner spotted it upon her return.

"You trying to sell sumthin'?" A teenage girl slouched on the top step, staring at him from the porch of the neighboring shotgun.

Moses crossed the postage stamp sized yard to the side fence. "I'm looking for Violet Boudreaux. I was hoping she could help me find some information on a case I'm working."

"You a POlice Man? Miss Violet - she don't ever do nothin' wrong. She's a teacher."

"Not police." He wanted to erase any doubt she might have about talking with him. "I work for an organization and we're researching some musicians. I understand Violet's grandmother was a blues singer."

"You mean Miss Mabel? She been gone over a year."

"When is the best time for me to find Miss Violet home?"

Already bored with the conversation, the girl shrugged

her shoulders. "My mama said she took li'l Joe and went to the country to visit relatives." She mumbled, her grimace showing she wasn't happy about the next fact, "School starts next week. So I guess she got to be back soon."

"Thanks for your help," smiled Moses, "I left my card and phone number on her door. If you see her, would you tell her I hope she calls?"

"I suppose."

Her unenthusiastic response probably meant she would forget about him by the time he turned the corner to his car. If he didn't hear from Violet tomorrow, he'd stop by again the day after.

♫

His GPS routed him to Larry Nash's address in Norco by way of Airline Highway. Originally built as a more direct route than the River Road between New Orleans and Baton Rouge, the road was aptly named since both Louis Armstrong International Airport and Baton Rouge Metropolitan Airport are along the highway. Most of its initial construction was completed during the Governorship of Huey P. Long who had advocated for a modern highway system. Although there had been some effort to clean up the highway's notorious history due to seedy hotels and motels which once lined it, the section he drove today was a dreary drive lined with tired looking industrial and abandoned buildings.

Once home to sugar cane plantations, Moses observed that the small town of Norco now owed its spot on the map to oil and gas refineries with their holding tanks and belching smoke from the distillation process.

He followed the navigator's instructions, turning onto a road where, according to the faded plywood sign, he was entering Possum Trailer Court. He drove slowly down the gravel lane which formed an upside down U, stopping at the last address on record for Nash. A large, ancient travel trailer with buckled siding and aluminum foil covered windows sat dejected on the lot. He pulled into the empty driveway where weeds fought for space among the rocks. The grass surrounding the RV hadn't been mowed in a while.

The place look deserted, but he knocked on the door anyway. The foil covered windows revealed nothing on his walk around the trailer. Quiet. No sound from inside either. He circled back, banged his palm on the metal exterior wall and loudly called out Nash's name.

"Ain't nobody home." The raspy voice came from a neighboring mobile home behind him. Moses spun, spying a woman lounging in a folding lawn chair, her fingers waving a lit cigarette. Dressed in one of those flowered housecoats which bigger women favored, dyed black hair wound in pink sponge curlers, it was difficult to judge her age or her friendliness. She said nothing further, just staring at him.

Moses attempted charm, thinking of the two aunts who raised him. Gravel crunched under his boots when he crossed the driveway. He smiled and introduced himself, "My name is Moses Martine. I hoped to find Larry Nash."

"Hmmph" she grunted, blowing the acrid smoke out the corner of her mouth, but offering no further comment.

Imagining she wasn't a fan of Nash and hoping she enjoyed gossip, he tried again. "I'm a private investigator and this is the last address we have on file for Mr. Nash. Does he or Phyllis still reside here?"

She scratched her arm and with what sounded more like a snort than a laugh, she said, "Man, where did you get your info? Phyllis has been gone for almost two years. She finally got smart and left before that bastard put her in the hospital."

Patiently, he asked, "So does Larry Nash still live here?"

After a long drag while she considered what to say, she

waved the cigarette at the empty lawn chair near her, inviting him to sit. "Would you like a cold one?" she asked, tapping an open cooler with her foot.

Moses started to decline thinking she meant beer, but after a quick glance at the ice chest, he grabbed an iced tea beverage. "Thank you." He reminded her of his question. "Does Larry Nash live next door?"

She stubbed the smoldering butt out in a clay flower pot filled with sand. "I guess he does. Old Man Possum says he can't remove that eyesore off the pad because Larry is still paying his rent. But I haven't seen him around here for six months or I would have told him to clean up his lot. Is he in trouble again?"

His head cocked to one side in contemplation, Moses said, "I don't really know him. He popped up in the middle of a case and since I don't trust coincidences, I wanted to check him out. Get some background on him. How long have you known him? What kind of friends does he have?"

She said, "He's been in this trailer court for about five years. I'm not sure he has any real friends. He used to drink with his work buddies from the refinery. He could get mean when he drank. Would take it out on Phyllis some nights. Then he quit the refinery. Said he got a better job - protecting and driving a big shot in New Orleans." She guffawed, "What does a skinny, mean man know about protection? He's probably just a driver and said that to make hisself sound more important."

Pausing to light another cigarette, she debated what she would say next. After a short silence, "Local gossip says he starting hanging around with a couple of sleazebags who bragged about doing extra work for the Italian Mafia."

"Have any names you want to share?" asked Moses.

"They're not from around here. I didn't recognize any of them." She shrugged. "Not sure how reliable that talk is. Could just be an exaggeration sprouted from the gossip grapevine, you know?"

Moses stood his empty bottle next to the cooler. Pushing himself up from the web lawn chair, he handed the lady his business card. "If Nash returns, I'd appreciate a call. Thank you for your time and hospitality. I didn't get your name."

His card disappeared into a pocket of her housecoat. After a silent beat, she said "Lupe. Lupe Perez. You take care, Mr. Martine."

17

WAREHOUSE DISTRICT: *protocol and etiquette*

Hawke made a u-turn on Lafayette Street, stopping in front of a two story battleship grey stucco building with black shutters. Large arched windows graced the ground floor while the second story sported a balcony with a delicate wrought iron railing and ornamental plaster cornice. In the aftermath of Katrina, Grandmother Esme moved her business to the Warehouse District. An architectural firm and accounting firm shared the first level. The Delahaye Academy of Etiquette and Protocol took up the entire second floor.

"You go on up. It shouldn't be hard for me to find a parking space for this little thing," Hawke said, referring to Echo's Smart Car. "We'll meet after your class."

She climbed the short flight of stairs from the lobby. A short, slender woman with light brown hair smiled with genuine pleasure when Echo pushed open the glass door into the reception area. Millie had been the Academy's receptionist for as long as Echo could remember. Leaning over the counter, she kissed Millie on the top of her head then started toward her training room.

"Tell Grandmother I'll see her after class."

"Ok, dear." Millie said in a sweet little voice. In a loud whisper she asked, "Is it true there's a treasure linked to Billy Williams?" Unlike Esme, Millie admitted a curiosity, blatantly interested in all the details of the Foundation's mystery-solving adventures.

On the way past Millie's desk to her class, Echo winked and whispered back, "It did create some amusing publicity during the festival weekend. The treasure is a wild rumor, Millie, but Zetta is trying to uncover the blogger's identity."

Twelve and thirteen year old girls assembled in the expansive room which was arranged to resemble various social settings. A conversational group of chairs. Sectional couch with coffee table. A round dinner table. Even a bar with stools. Used for different parts of the Corporate Etiquette and Protocol curriculum, Echo preferred holding her session here instead of the classic school room. The teens were less tense in this informal set up.

Although this course was offered to males and females, rarely did a boy elect to participate in the program sponsored by the Foundation. Some of the girls in this group came from housing projects with no father figure in their lives. Others from low income immigrant families whose parents were not fluent in English. One girl's mother died last year. Her father worked rotation shifts offshore so she shuffled back and forth between her dad and aunt. "Good afternoon, Mrs. LaBauve," chorused the young girls.

"Good afternoon, girls. Relax," said Echo. She retrieved her tablet, setting her bag on a small console table, waiting for the girls to settle into their chosen seats.

With a kind smile, she reminded them, "Relax. Don't slouch." *How many times had she heard that from her grandmother?*

She wirelessly connected her computer tablet to the projector. A few nervous twitters sounded when a picture of a juvenile appeared on the screen at the front of the room. Dressed in a blue plaid uniform skirt and white blouse, the young girl stood in a stiff pose with her arms hanging at her side, abrasions on her cheek and forehead, long curls frayed from a scuffle. The students studied the photo more closely, observing the girl's hands balled in tight fists, her jaw tensed.

"This is me when I was thirteen years old," announced Echo catching the class' attention.

After her parents' death, her grandparents agreed Echo would stay with Poppy until she entered the eighth grade, after which she would live with her paternal grandmother in New Orleans to attend Mount Carmel Catholic School. Somewhat relieved, she had thought, *My thirteenth birthday is a long way away.* She loved Grandmother, but Victoria's adventurous determination didn't exasperate Poppy like it sometimes did Grandmother Esme.

She wasn't sure what had prompted Esme to take that picture. It seemed out of character for her grandmother, who preferred to memorialize what Echo referred to as her 'dress-up' moments.

Lost in her own reverie, her silence masqueraded as a dramatic pause. She mustered a poise her grandmother would be proud of and continued, "I believe we can all find the self-confidence to rise above disadvantages -real or imagined- in our lives. I'd like to tell you a story."

When she accepted Esme's ultimatum that she must personally facilitate a class in order for the Academy to host a program for the Foundation, she first fretted about it, then meditated on her own memories of being that age. Other instructors taught the girls etiquette survival - the art of good manners and conversational skills while Echo used storytelling to articulate typical teenage insecurities and conflicts.

Echo discovered her talent for conscious dream control soon after that picture was taken. Her self-awareness grew as she interacted with her own subconscious mind via dream characters. Not everyone could develop the skill of lucid dreaming, manipulating their imaginary experiences with a knowledge that they can make choices inside their dream – a virtual reality where anything they conceive comes true. Echo worked hard to demonstrate to the girls how to project who they wanted to be and how to affect outcomes.

Through practice, Echo had perfected the telling of her story with emphasis, humor and empathy, discovering that many of her students related to the stubborn, frizzy-haired thirteen-year-old staring out from the screen with a pained, slightly confused look in her eyes.

Her only prop, photos of herself at different states of youth, assisted in telling the story of a young girl who lost her parents at age nine, adapted to an idyllic life with her Poppy, to then be tragically thrust into a totally foreign environment – Mount Carmel Catholic School where she was the strange outsider. And let's not forget the pressure of being Esme Delahaye's granddaughter, disappointing anyone who expected her to be a mini Emily Post.

Her story was really a parable about accepting different personal facets and adapting. She wanted the girls to know they were not doomed to or constricted by their current environment. Nor did they need to choose one environment to the exclusion of another.

At the end of the session, after her students left the room, Echo plopped into a chair, taking a few minutes to herself. No matter how many times she told this story, the first photo used to startle the girls into attention also brought bittersweet memories of that day in the school yard when some girls called her a white witch. Now she realized it was fear of what they didn't understand that had triggered their name calling, ostracizing the new girl in class. Her Grandmother had shown uncommon perception taking her home and calling Poppy to visit. The picture represented an inflection point in her life - where Echo began learning how to adapt and blend without abandoning her own individuality.

She switched off the lights and walked back across the reception area to meet Hawke, who was speaking with Esme and a pretty petite blonde. Not wanting to interrupt their conversation, she brushed her lips on her grandmother's cheek and stood quietly by her side until the blonde completed what she was saying. Esme smiled and made introductions.

"This is Alicia Silverman. She's participating in our Protocol Training. Alicia is married to Martin Silverman. Alicia, this is my granddaughter, Victoria."

Flipping her fair hair back over her shoulder, she said, "Everyone calls me Allie. And, honey I know who you are. Victoria LaBauve, aka Echo. My golfing club loves reading about your juicy mysteries. We were fans of your investigative column." Alicia looked at least ten years younger than her husband. "We wish you'd start a blog about your mystery adventures."

Echo extended her hand. "I met your husband briefly on Sunday after the Jazz Mass, but didn't get a chance to speak to you."

"Maybe we'll have more time to visit at the Audubon fundraising gala Thursday night," gushed Alicia. "I helped Esme on the Auction Committee, but I'm looking for other opportunities to contribute in the community and I find your Benevolent Foundation fascinating."

At the mention of the Foundation, Esme interrupted, redirecting the conversation, "We've collected some very nice items for the Gala's silent auction. Thank you, Hawke, for your contribution. I'm sure your photograph will be a popular item, as always."

Hawke reached his arm out and hugged Esme close to him, dropping a kiss on the top of her perfectly coiffed hair. "You're welcome, Esme. Victoria and I are supportive of the Audubon Association."

He switched his attention back to Alicia, addressing her desire for more community involvement. "You should check out the Broadway South project which the Foundation has contributed to. They are looking for volunteers and your husband might also be interested in it from its economic development perspective."

Echo asked Alicia, "Your husband's a councilman, isn't he?"

With a relaxed grin, Alicia replied, "Yes. He is now, but Martin is thinking about running for a state political office."

She revealed, lowering her girlish voice, "Martin's first name is really Tilden." Giggling, she said "He goes by his middle name rather than be called Tilden the Third." Then in a tone appropriate for a politician's wife, probably learned in her protocol class, she continued, "The Stanton and Silverman partnership began with their fathers."

FLASH! Initials. TMS.

"Mrs. Silverman, your car is downstairs at the curb."

"Thank you, Millie. Well, I shouldn't keep my husband's driver waiting. Echo and Hawke, I look forward to spending more time with you both." Giving them a small fingertip wave goodbye, she walked out.

"Martin thought the Protocol Training would help prepare her for a political campaign." Esme sighed. "She's such a sweet, uncomplicated person. I worry about her stamina for the world of politics."

"What do you know about Martin Silverman and Theodore Stanton?"

"The Stanton family has been prominent in New Orleans since the 1800's. Their wealth started in property and later, expanded to oil. The Stantons are influential and involved in the community with multiple generations holding political positions."

"Tilden Silverman the First married the daughter of a Chicago family whose money was in railroads. Tilden Silverman the Second moved from Chicago to New Orleans at the height of railroad construction in Louisiana. When the railroads brought lumbermen, Silverman added timber to the family business. The Silverman family gained prominence when they extended their empire into New Orleans property and shipping in the early 1900s. Martin is the first in his family to hold a political office."

"I wonder how their families became business partners." Echo mused.

"I believe it was in the early or mid-forties," said Esme. "Stanton Senior was much older than Silverman. Until ten years ago, Teddy's partner was Martin's father, Tilden the Second."

Two old families, prominent at the time of Billy's photo. She had flashed on Teddy and Martin. Both have been inquisitive about Archer's mystery key. Her instinct humming, Echo asked her grandmother, "What is Teddy Stanton's full name?"

"Theodore Montgomery Stanton. His father was named Thomas Montgomery Stanton. For some reason, they referred to them as Senior and Junior when his father was alive, even though they have different first names."

"How coincidental." Echo thought aloud, "They both have the initials TMS."

"The same as the monogram on that cigarette case," chimed in Millie from behind her desk.

Piqued by Millie's observation, Esme hesitated in confusion, "What cigarette case?"

After Hawke recounted a brief summary of Archer's mystery, Esme didn't attempt to hide her annoyance."Victoria, you can't possibly consider the coincidence of a monogram a salient fact for your little mystery."

She glared at Echo with reproachful eyes, not giving her a chance to respond. Ice crystals wrapped her words. "These are prominent, well respected families. You can't accuse them, even in speculation. Of what? For all you know, that key is a sentimental memory of a music box."

Echo felt an instant squeezing hurt, her composure a fragile shell. The warmth of Hawke's hand stroking the small of her back stilled her shift into a warrior princess stance. She relaxed her arms, raised her chin and with all the dignity she could muster said, "Grandmother, you know I will do what is right."

18

ROYAL STREET: *the cat and fiddle*

"I found obituaries for both of the men named by Archer's old-timers. It's impossible to tell from the pics posted with the obituaries if one of them is the fifth person in Billy's photo. Neither of them had surviving wives or children."

Zetta continued, "Unless we find something more about them tomorrow in the archives, I suggest they are a dead-end and not going to help us solve our mystery."

Wrinkling her nose at her reflection in the mirror, Echo changed out of her skirt back into her blue pants and shirt, and called out, "Any *helpful* discoveries, oh master of information?"

Zetta's eyes crinkled with suppressed laughter. "Maybe not helpful, but definitely amusing. Billy's treasure appears to be quickly developing into a local legend without any concern for evidence."

A hodgepodge of screen shots jumped up on the wall screen. Zetta's stylus danced on her tablet.

"It's hard to determine the origin, but I think the

sequence is facebook, blogger, newspaper. Someone commented on our facebook page about the photo but no mention of a key. I can't figure out how the blogger picked up on the theme of Billy's key leading to treasure, but then someone commented on the blog about Billy's finishing carpentry ability and surmised he built a secret compartment in a place people would least suspect."

Her eyebrows lifted in curiosity, Echo asked, "And someone thought the place least suspected would be St Augustine Church?"

Zetta pointed to a blog entry. "This blogger dedicated a couple of days to ruminating about the items Archer found and their meaning." Enlarged on screen was a blog site. Emblazoned across the top was the title *The Cat and Fiddle*. It seems he created his own fairy tale about possible treasure and where it could be hidden – anywhere from in the church where Billy was a deacon to buried in the back yard."

"And as we can see from the newspaper article, people started searching for treasure based on nothing more than this blogger's fantasy ideas."

Echo brushed her curls away from her eyes and waved her forefinger in a circle quoting Dr Seuss, "*From there to here, and here to there, funny things are everywhere.*" Then with a question in her eyes, she said, "Humorous stuff this blog, but still only a distraction. What relevance does all this have to our mystery?"

Floosh, blamma, ptung. A colorful rubber band ball bounced on screen before a new entry appeared for *The Cat and Fiddle*. The headline read "Billy's Treasure Contest - $5,000 reward". Entrants were asked to suggest what they thought the key fit. If ever the key opened a lock, the entrant with the correct answer would win $5,000 cash.

"Wow. Is this guy stupid or does Mr. Cat have advertisers willing to pay the reward?" asked Zetta looking back over her shoulder.

FLASH! Her intuition hummed. Echo leaned her head back on the couch and closed her eyes to concentrate. Zetta sat, waiting quietly for her friend to rejoin their conversation.

Echo stood suddenly, energy crackling around her. "You're right, Zetta. Something is fishy about this contest." She asked, pointing to the screen, "Can you identify that blogger?"

Before Zetta could respond, Echo tapped an icon on her control panel then walked to the floor safe.

Two quick rings from the screen interrupted them. Moses' face with short stubble glanced out at them before quickly looking away, the sound of moving traffic in the background. "Bonjour, Madame and Mademoiselle. I hope you don't mind if I keep my eyes on the road. I'm at the six-ten split with drivers jockeying for position - all in a rush to be somewhere."

From where she knelt next to the safe, Zetta addressed Moses onscreen "Zetta will fill you in on a blogger and contest. This contest is suspiciously lame. Can you visit the blogger and find out who is funding the contest reward and why? My intuition is screaming. The persons responsible for breaking in Archer's store must be desperately looking for clues about the key."

"I'm at your command, Princess."

Echo removed the key and cigarette case from the safe. She stood, placed them in her bag and grabbed her cap.

"Where are you disappearing to?" asked Zetta with a pouting grimace. "We still haven't looked through Archer's boxes."

"I promise we'll inspect them as soon as I return. I'm walking up Royal to the antique shops. Maybe one of the shopkeepers can tell us if there is anything special about these two items."

Waving as she headed out the door, she called out to

Moses, "Hawke and I will join you at the club tonight after dinner. Stay safe."

A serious frown twisted Moses' face staring out from the wall screen. "Hawk is not going to be pleased that we let her waltz out alone with the case and key.

"What do you mean – *we* – kemosabe?" asked Zetta. "Aren't you the warden - oh, I mean guardian of her safety?"

He pounded his steering wheel in frustration. "He thinks she's safely tucked in at the Foundation until dinnertime."

"Chill, dude. She's just walking up Royal Street." She said facetiously, "Must've been an anomaly that Echo managed to take care of herself perfectly fine while you played ranger in the desert and Hawke traipsed jungles with his camera."

Zetta clicked her remote disconnecting him.

19

ROYAL STREET: *uncover or not?*

Echo dismissed the first three shops she walked past. Many of the Royal Street shop keepers were third and fourth generation antique business owners who knew the origin of their objects. The candelabra, snuff tins, and silver tea service displayed among a hodgepodge of items in the window of the fourth storefront suggested someone in this shop might be knowledgeable about small collectibles.

She squinted to readjust her eyes from the bright glare outdoors to the gloomy, low lit interior. Moving across the cool, concrete floor, Echo shivered with the thought that a hundred or more years of dark, sad experiences clung to many of the objects for sale causing the somber atmosphere in the antique store.

At the sound of the rattling cow bell, a small, hunchbacked woman looked up from the book she was reading. She planted her tiny feet on the floor, stilling her rocking chair, dark eyes set in a worn face patiently watching Echo walk towards the back of the shop. In a girlish voice which contradicted her wizened countenance, "Hello, dear.

What can I help you with?"

Echo wondered how the old lady knew she wanted help, then smiled sheepishly at herself. She was probably being oversensitive to a greeting the shopkeeper offered to all new customers.

She shook off the solemn feeling the somber atmosphere had triggered in her. Her eyes warm and at ease, she flashed an engaging smile and placed the cigarette case and key on the top of a display counter near where the woman sat. "I wondered if there is anything unique about either of these items that might help me identify the owner of the case or the type of lock this key would fit."

"Ahh, you are the keeper of Archer's find," said the shopkeeper rising from her rocker. Hunched over the display counter, she lifted the cigarette case, the skin on her hands paper thin and wrinkled. Echo gave the woman a direct stare with her clear green eyes, dipping her chin to acknowledge what the old lady said, but remained silent, waiting.

After tracing the monogram with a gnarled finger, the old woman replaced the silver case and picked up the key. Her hand trembled slightly as she held the key up, turning it into the light of an old pole lamp. Next she placed the head of the key between her teeth and bit down. Returning the key to the counter, she pointed first to the cigarette case.

"This cigarette case is silver and a common design for a man. I place it in the mid to late 1930s. The monogram is hand etched. See these scrolled hash marks in the lower part of the central S? They suggest this may be a distinctive family design – and if it is, it's possible to match this to other monogrammed family silver."

Excited, Echo asked, "Have you seen this specific monogram before?"

The shopkeeper shrugged her small rounded shoulders, "I don't know which family this belongs to. Most monograms were engraved from standard font styles. Sometimes marks were added to the standard – as this appears to be." With a slight sneer, she commented, "I guess some prominent people felt the need for further distinction."

Hopeful, nudging the key on the counter towards the shopkeeper, Echo asked, "Anything special about this?"

The old woman's thin lips broadened into a smile revealing small crooked teeth. "Yes. I think this is one-of-a-kind. Although this looks like a skeleton key which could open many locks, it was hand tooled to fit a specific lock." She held the key up for Echo to view the teeth more closely.

"It's made of pewter, not silver. Pewter is a softer material so easier to form the distinctive teeth design at the bottom of this shank. The shank is short so the lock is not very deep – probably locks a small container or drawer rather than something like a large trunk or door."

The old woman twirled the key admiring the intricate fleur de lis pattern of its head. "Whoever created this key is an artist. They had a talent for fine work and didn't trust their secret to a locksmith."

Echo thanked the shopkeeper for her help, placing the case and key back in her bag. She blinked away the peachy blur caused by touching the key. *Protect. Was the key protecting something that she wasn't supposed to uncover?*

As the old woman settled back into her rocker, she observed in her juvenile voice, "Must be a potent secret about a self-important person. Secrets tend to lose their power over time. Most common folk wouldn't care about old news coming to light."

Hmmm, thought Echo on her walk back to the Foundation. *That blogger has people hunting treasure while whoever broke into Archer's store is concerned with keeping a secret from being exposed. Why would someone incent the blogger to encourage treasure hunting if that same person wants to protect a secret?*

A prickling along her spine pulled her back from her reverie, instantly alerting her that she was in danger. She ducked into the next open doorway, walked through the souvenir shop, emerging from a second door which opened onto the street corner. Echo touched an icon on her phone and started sweeping, capturing images on Royal Street with her camcorder app.

None of the pedestrians slowed or showed an unusual interest in her. Traffic moved freely. There! A dirty white truck with tinted windows pulled sharply to the curb, idling. Echo walked back towards the truck, all the while capturing the truck on her phone's camera. Chrome bumpers with rust dimples aged it. The windows were tinted much darker than regulations allowed, blocking her from seeing the driver, so she decided to walk up to the car to knock on the window. Maybe the person was just waiting for someone but she doubted it. When she neared the front bumper, the driver revved its engine and swerved out into traffic, barely escaping a collision with another car. Startled drivers honked in retaliation.

Echo ran up the sidewalk chasing the truck. The truck made an abrupt left turn at the corner and sped away before Echo was able to capture its license plate.

Someone was following her.

She forwarded the video from her phone to the Foundation's server. Maybe Zetta could work some magic and find something useful about the truck or driver.

20

Faubourg Marigny: *the blogger*

Moses drove up Burgundy, crossing Elysian Fields Avenue, named after the Champs-Élysées in Paris. He recalled that once Washington Square area was nicknamed "Little Angola" because of the criminals there. The reggae band jamming on the street corner right outside of the Book Nook which sat next door to a tattoo parlor was just a tip of the bustling bohemian scene the Faubourg Marigny neighborhood had become. Frenchmen Street had exploded in popularity with tourists for its eclectic venues of music and bar food.

Using her tech research skills -which Moses avoided knowing too much about- Zetta had shadowed The Cat and Fiddle blogger until she discovered a name. Andrew Garwood.

Bought, sold, renovated, neglected year in, year out, the shotgun houses lining the street are part of New Orleans' architectural heritage. In its most rudimentary design, the shotgun is a one-room-wide house without halls. One repeated theory is the name stemmed from the fact that you could shoot a gun through the house from front to back, though that's debatable, since the doors often aren't arranged in a straight line. What is more certain is that the design fit snugly on the twenty-five foot wide lots unique to New Orleans.

He watched the front of a cabbage green camelback shotgun raised three feet off the ground from where he sat in his car. The physical address in the Bywater area which Zetta traced from the blogger's IP address was a clone of other houses like it on the street. Concrete steps led up to a shallow porch. The two tall windows on one side were trimmed with blue-green louvered shutters to match the door. The houses were mostly distinguished by bold painted colors although a few boasted lush gardens in the front yards which were no larger than a pillow slip.

Besides a couple of boys rollerblading, the street was quiet. Traffic would pick up soon with families returning home from their workdays. Moses wondered if Andrew Garwood worked during the day and blogged at night or maybe he worked nights and blogged during the day, since Zetta said he had posted a reward earlier today.

He stepped out of his Jeep, crossed the street and climbed the steps. His thick fist knocked hard on the blue-green door. He immediately heard someone inside. A safety chain kept the door from opening more than three inches, but that was enough for him to see the woman's plump face peeking through the crack. A dog's snout pushed into the space giving Moses a sniff test for danger.

"Yes?" the woman asked hesitantly, slight apprehension on her face.

Moses smiled to reassure the woman. He handed her his business card then opened his wallet to display his Private Investigator license. Anyone could make up an identification which looked official, but somehow this tended to gain people's confidence – convince them he wasn't there to rob them, or worse.

"My name is Moses Martine and I work for a Foundation which is researching a musician. I was told Andrew Garwood, who writes the blog 'The Cat and the Fiddle', lives here."

The woman read the card again, bit her lip and stared back at Moses.

"Mrs. Garwood, if possible I'd like to speak with your husband, Andrew. I think he may have some information helpful to our investigation. I promise he's not in trouble and I won't take much of his time."

The lady shouted up the stairs behind her, "Andrew, come down here. Someone's here to see you."

When she reopened the door after removing the safety chain, a lanky boy with tousled hair who appeared about sixteen years old stood behind her. "I'm Trisha Garwood and this is my son, Andrew."

Surprised, Moses thought, *this kid caused all the hoopla about the treasure?*

Remaining cautious, Mrs. Garwood stepped out onto the porch pulling the boy after her. "Let's talk outside." The dog's paws slipped and slided on the hard wood floor as he scurried out with them.

Andrew asked, "What's going on?"

Moses responded, "You've created some excitement with your recent blogs. I wondered how you learned about Billy William's key."

Andrew sat down on the top step, rubbing his hands over his face as if to wake himself up. He stared up at Moses and said, "Well, first there was that little article in the newspaper about that young guy, Archer, finding something when his great-uncle's house was demolished. I didn't think anything about it until I heard from a friend that the pretty red-headed lady with the *woo-woo* abilities was looking for other clues about the stuff."

Moses grinned at the woo-woo comment. Joining Andrew on the top step, he asked, "What friend did you hear this from?"

Andrew pointed his thumb sideways to a purple house. "Stoogie next door plays drums at a Jazz club on Bourbon. He said the lady showed pictures of a key that looked special made and maybe she was investigating because the key led to some kind of treasure. That gave me the idea for my blog. Special key means special lock means special stash."

Moses thought the kid was telling the truth. He knew Stoogie, the drummer in the group Echo had questioned on Friday night at the club.

Embarrassed, the boy looked up from under the hair flopping over his forehead. "Are you here cuz all those people invaded that man's property and church? I'm really sorry. I didn't mean for that to happen."

Concerned, his mother spoke up, "Mr. Martine, if you are here to-."

Moses interrupted, quickly reassuring her. "I'm not here to accuse your son of anything. I was hoping he could help me."

He turned back to Andrew and asked, "What's the deal with the $5,000 reward?"

Astonished, his mother asked "What $5,000 reward?"

"Uh-oh." Andrew hunched his shoulders and hung his head.

"Andrew, what $5,000?" Mrs. Garwood's voice rose in confused anger and frustration.

He mumbled, "I thought I could buy that guitar I've been saving for." His bottom lip trembled. "Instead I'm mixed up with some crazy person in something I can't get out of. Mister Moses, I didn't know what to do."

One look at his mother's peeved expression told Moses

this probably wasn't the first time the boy would have to work at explaining his way back into her good grace.

Ever the peacekeeper, he said quietly, "Why don't you tell me about that."

21

ROYAL STREET: *unsolved murder*

The video captured by Echo's phone rolled before them on the big wall screen. "Plain white truck. Dry muddy sides. Rusted, pitted bumpers." Zetta sighed, declaring "There is nothing to distinguish this truck from hundreds of other older model trucks."

Echo exhaled a deep breath, disappointed. "Is that the news you had me rush back for?"

Making a raspberry sound with her lips, Zetta rattled off, "No. I had you rush back so I'd know you were safe and Moses could breathe again, knowing Hawke wouldn't kill him if something happened to you."

Not giving Echo a chance to respond, Zetta pointed a crooked forefinger and simulated a Yoda expression, saying, "Faith in your girl genius, you must have."

She clicked her remote showing footage sneaked from traffic cams outside their alley's iron gate. "I don't think you're imagining being watched. Notice the dirty white truck with dark windows. It drives past the gate several times on Saturday afternoon. No sign of the same truck during the time the alarm went off Saturday night. The only vehicle which passes more than once is this motorcycle."

Before Echo asked, Zetta said, "We only get a side view of the truck so no license plate number. The motorcycle is illegally operating without a license plate."

"But here's the pièce de résistance," Zetta trilled. Footage from a different traffic cam appeared onscreen.

"This silver town car was parked for a while on Friday morning a block away from Archer's store soon after the break-in. Although its occupants aren't visible from this angle, the license plate is registered to Stanton and Silverman Commercial Properties."

Echo sat in her anchor state – legs crossed Indian style, each hand pinching an earlobe. She stared into space deeply relaxed, allowing her thoughts to flow in random patterns.

In anticipation of what came next, Zetta opened a blank document and activated recording mode, ready to capture Echo's ruminations.

"TMS. Theodore Montgomery Stanton and Tilden Martin Silverman."

"Teddy Stanton still wears monograms- his handkerchief."

"Was it coincidence that Stanton attended Hawke's art showing?"

"Flash of anxiety and anger from Silverman at the Jazz Mass."

"Silverman's interest in the objects and what we might have discovered."

"Silverman seen with Nash."

"Potent secret about self-important person."

She dropped her hands into her lap, focusing her exotic shaped eyes on Zetta.

"From a statistical perspective, coincidences are inevitable," said Zetta. Continuing her Yoda impression, "But coincidence here, I think not."

"Agreed," said Echo. "Let's work on the assumption that either Stanton or Silverman is involved and figure out why before someone gets hurt." She sighed, "If only I could get a peek at their family silver, I might know who to focus on – Stanton or Silverman."

Zetta held her head, imitating a headache. "Girl, Esme would so not approve."

"Let's get these out of the way," said Zetta, placing the boxes from Archer on the cypress table. She pushed one box towards Echo and kept one for herself. "What exactly are we looking for?"

"A map with directions to the lock that the key fits would be nice," teased Echo. "Since that's not probable, maybe a picture of the white man with his name inscribed on the back."

They worked in silence for a while sifting through the boxes.

Holding up a photo, Zetta said, "Billy and Sister Mabel is written on the back of this one."

In the photo, Billy had his arm around Mabel's shoulders while she held a box wrapped in a bow.

"Maurice said Billy made a wooden box for Mabel." Peering closer at the picture, Echo said, "You can't tell if there is a lock on the box." She laid the picture on a small stack they had separated for further review.

A few minutes later, she uncovered a half page torn from an old newspaper dated March 1940.

The torn page had been folded so that one of the articles was prominent. Luciano "Lucky" Scarmuzzi was found shot to death in an alley behind the Open Door Club. The police had no leads and speculated whether the motive was robbery since the man's wallet and watch were missing. There were no witnesses and no weapon was found at the scene. Mr.

Scarmuzzi had worked security and managed musician bookings for some of the local Jazz clubs before his death. The article did not identify any specific employer.

"Wonder why Billy Williams kept this?" Echo placed it with the other photos in the short stack of interest on the cypress table. Her senses hummed.

"Hmmm." Echo cocked her head in consideration. She picked up the clipping for a closer inspection.

"Zetta, does this look like the man in the suit?"

The original of the five people in the club materialized on the wall screen. Zetta took the clipping from Echo, looking from clipping to screen, comparing the images.

Absorbed in her comparison, Zetta absently rubbed her forefinger up and down the bridge of her nose. "Hard to tell, comparing this frontal shot with that man's side profile – but they sure look like the same person to me."

"Well if the man in the suit is this Luciano Scarmuzzi, the cigarette case isn't his. So what's the thread that connects the dead man, TMS monogram and key?" asked Echo.

"This guy booked musicians. Billy's been described as protecting the musicians from the graft. Is it possible Billy shot Scarmuzzi and hid the gun?"

Doubt in her eyes, Echo said, "Doesn't sound like the Billy described in the articles or memorialized by Maurice's daddy. Could he have hidden the gun to protect someone else? Then why not just throw it in the river?"

22

French Quarter: *stolen moon*

Following an early supper of spicy gumbo and warm crusty French bread, Hawke and Echo relaxed on a bench at the far end of the grassy area of Woldenberg Park. A skinny elastic headband held Echo's cinnamon red waves away from her face, falling freely to her shoulders. Savoring the intimate respite, Hawke brushed the hair off her neck, idly twirling a curl around his finger. They watched in consensual silence the sparse river traffic. He cherished these serene intervals of time with Victoria – no matter how transient.

A single tugboat shepherded an assembly of flat bottom barges riding high in the river – five barges tied together, three abreast. A muted horn tooted in the distance signaling the ferry departure from Algiers Point to traverse the Mississippi River's natural crescent, its destination the Canal Street landing. The month of August still boasts more daylight than night hours; but at seven forty-seven as rays broke through a thin haze below billowing grey clouds, a weird blueish sunset subdued the day.

Her shoulders rose, then fell as she took a deep cleansing breath. "Borrowing from a wine connoisseur's lexicon, this day was full-bodied and slightly acidic," Echo said.

Hawke stood, tweaking the hair wrapped around his finger, "I know where we can find you a red wine to match your day."

♫♪

"Hawke! Echo!" A young man, attired in a red jacket, black bow tie and top hat, called from atop the driver's bench seat.

Hawke and Echo descended the steps, stopping next to the carriage parked on Decatur Street. Jerome had worked several jobs —one of them as a bartender at the Sunset Riff— until he saved enough cash to buy and refurbish the single carriage he now proudly perched in. The older tour guides, having converted to double carriages, targeted groups of tourists. Jerome, the youngest carriage driver in the quarter, aimed his sales pitch at couples, touting the romance of his carriage ride. He worked to enchant his customers with colorful facts and genuine enthusiasm, often not demonstrated in the tired, drone of the standard tour guide spiel.

"How's it going, Jerome?" asked Hawke, patting the mule's flank.

The mule snorted and stamped his back leg. He shook his head, his pointed ears at attention.

"Uhm. You might want to be careful there," Jerome said, pointing to his light-faced brown mule who wore a matching black top hot. "He still has mulish reactions to some things. He's a young mule, still learning the ways of the street," he explained. "I only take customers at night right now, when there's less traffic - which means less chance he'll try to race a

139

car."

"I thought mules were stubborn and didn't run," said Echo with a laugh.

Jerome pulled at his bottom lip with his forefinger and thumb, a habit he probably didn't realize he had. He responded seriously to Echo's comment, "Mules tend to be better sprinters than distance runners and more difficult to control."

"Mr. Butler and I need to spend more time during the next couple of weeks practicing – getting him accustomed to his street walk during the day."

He pointed to a piece of the horse tack -black plastic cups attached to the bridle- to prevent the mule from seeing to the side. "The winkers work for most distractions, but he has the darndest reaction to the revving sound of an engine alongside him. He tries to break into a run as if he senses competition."

Jerome raised his hand, the reins grasped in his fist, "Let me and Mr. Butler give you a ride to where you're going."

With a gallant sweep, Hawke's lean, muscular arms lifted Victoria up into the white carriage. He used the short step to climb in next to her onto the red tufted leather seat, wrapping his arm around her shoulder pulling her close to him in a sheltering gesture. His compelling coffee eyes, firm features and confident set to his shoulders intimated a masculine protectiveness.

Hawke retreated in reverie, lulled by the movement and slight bounce of the carriage on its springs. The tlot-tlot, tlot-tlot sound of the mule's hooves on asphalt resembled the beat of a heart. His handsome face stared up at the quarter moon high overhead in the cloudy, starless sky. He stroked the soft flesh of Echo's arm and asked, "Did I ever tell you the story of the Coyote and the Moon?"

Echo snuggled closer, resting her head back against Hawke's arm, to view the moon – more than one-half enshrouded in darkness. "I don't think so."

Relishing this tranquil moment, with a warm smile, he recited the story learned from his mother.

Once there was no Moon because someone had stolen it. The people asked "Who will be the Moon?" The Yellow Fox agreed to give it a try but he was so bright it made the Earth hot at night. Then the people asked Coyote to try and he agreed. The Coyote was a good moon, not too bright - not too dim. But from his vantage point in the sky the Coyote could see what everyone was doing. Whenever he saw someone doing something dishonest he would shout "HEY! That person is stealing meat from the drying racks!" or "HEY! That person is cheating at the moccasin game!" Finally, the people who wished to do things in secret got together and said "Coyote is too noisy. Let's take him out of the sky." So someone else became the moon. Coyote can no longer see what everyone else is doing but he still tries to snoop into everyone else's business.

A loud boisterous laugh could be heard from the carriage driver's seat.

The heartbeat sound of the mule's hooves silenced. The carriage halted in front of the Royal Sonesta's entrance on Bourbon Street.

Jerome turned in his seat. "Welcome to your destination." He grabbed the opportunity to practice his memorized historical facts saying, "Did you know that this sight once held a vinegar factory and a winery? The American Brewing Company bought the winery in 1890. By 1960, the buildings had fallen into disrepair and were demolished to make room for this hotel. The new owners hired an architect to design this exterior to look like typical 1830s New Orleans row houses."

After Hawke assisted Echo down from the carriage, she planted her feet on the sidewalk, her shoulders squared in a defensive posture. "Was your story supposed to be a parable for me?"

"Relax, my warrior princess. It's nothing more than a story - an old Indian lore triggered by the sight of the moon tonight."

Hawke ushered her into the low lit Sunset Riff, aware of the sexual tension building between them. His steady gaze bore into her in expectation. Echo leaned into him and Hawke moved his mouth over hers, in a slow drugging kiss. "One drink with Moses, then you and I can continue this at home."

♫♫

"So an anonymous e-mailer – the fixer – initially offered the kid $5,000 to generate interest in the mystery of the key. But, then," laughed Moses, "they were astounded when strangers started digging for a treasure. So the kid gets another email. They don't want people searching for treasure. They want to contain the blog discussion to ideas or leads on what the key might open given that it was from the 1940s."

Hawke finger combed his loose hair off his brow. "That's like trying to push toothpaste back in the tube after you squeezed too much," he commented. "Impossible."

Unfolding a printout of an email, Moses flattened the page down on the low table in front of Echo. "They threatened the safety of his mother if he didn't follow their instructions, hence the latest blog offering a reward."

Echo fidgeted on the burgundy leather cushion where she huddled with Moses and Hawke in the far corner. Soft jazz played over the speakers. The first live music set wouldn't begin for another half hour.

She swirled the ruby wine, trying hard to detect the aroma of wet leaves. *Nope. She would just take Hawke's word for it.* She swallowed, the persistent flavor of the earthy French wine lingered in her mouth.

"Whoever is behind this must know or suspect what the

key is hiding but they don't have a clue what the key fits or where whatever it opens is stashed."

Sometimes questions are more important than answers, she read the quote on the napkin. "Well, here's a question. Why take the risk of stirring up all this attention?"

"There wouldn't even be a mystery if they hadn't broken into Archer's store," Hawke said. "Archer would have worn the key as a pendant in oblivion and delegated the cigarette case to a curiosity."

Moses lounged back on the curved banquet seat, arms folded across his chest. "To answer your question, Echo, the cost of exposure if someone else finds what's hidden must be greater than the risk of the attention."

Just as Echo finished telling the events of her day, all three phones buzzed simultaneously - followed by a more insistent siren whirring from Echo's tablet.

23

The Foundation: *bobble head*

"Lights, depart." The recessed ceiling lights dimmed at her voice command, leaving the rest of the office in darkness. Zetta's prideful voice echoed in the empty office. "Mr. Earl, you and I have achieved a most excellent integrated relationship which I do believe transcends my initial infatuation with you." She giggled to herself.

The words *Mr. Earl* triggered the computer's voice command system. An animated short Cajun man sitting in a pirogue in the swamp appeared. "Command, you say?"

"Command, none. Just playing around, I say."

Inspired by Echo's unyielding loyalty and respect for her wise old mentor, Zetta selected the guardian of the newspaper archives as the computer's namesake. The voice command system did not differentiate between voices so she had cleverly trained the system commands in Yoda-speak - an unconventional, yet sufficient security measure.

Noting the time, she thought *I'll have to grab a late supper after rehearsal.* Zetta punched in her security code and stepped out into the twilight of the courtyard. Before her hand reached the scan plate, someone grabbed the ruffled neck of her blouse yanking her backwards. A black gloved hand clamped over her mouth before she could scream. Zetta twisted her head attempting to break the grasp.

"Stop that." The hand yanked her head back to get her attention. In a harsh low tone, her attacker said, "Just do what I say and you won't be hurt."

She stilled.

"Good girly." He herded her back inside the Foundation office, kicking the front door closed behind them. The man kept his grasp on her shirt, maintaining his position out of sight behind her.

Her mind raced through scenarios and probabilities. The alarm wouldn't be triggered, but the video should be running. She looked at the back wall to confirm the tiny blinking light on the lower left of the blank screen. In the low light, she could see a reflection of the man behind her. *Lord, it was a bobble head spaceman!* Her breaths came faster and deeper. Aware she was on the verge of hyperventilating; she closed her eyes and focused on slowing her breathing like she had seen Echo practice. She glanced back at the reflection. *Ok. That's more like it. He's wearing a white motorcycle helmet and his head is moving - scanning the room.*

"Where are they?" He removed his hand from her mouth.

"Who are you looking for?" asked Zetta stiffly.

"Not who. What."

"Hey guy, I'm not a mind reader. What are you searching for? This is just an office space." Pretty sure this wasn't a common robbery, she offered anyway, "We don't keep money here."

The shake he gave her rattled her jaw. "I heard you're a

very smart girl so don't act stupid with me."

He pushed her around the room, searching. He grabbed the small stack of photos and newspaper clipping from the driftwood table, shoving them into his jacket pocket.

"I'm guessing you have them locked in a safe here." A hard object pressed into her shoulder. His voice sneered, "Don't be a stubborn dumbass. If you want to play with your friends again, you're going to open the safe without drama and give me the key and case."

When she didn't respond, he said, "I promise I'll let you go if you just give me what I need."

This is the place in all the movies where you're not supposed to believe the bad guy.

"Over here." Her voice squeaked. She took a tentative step sideways. He moved with her. She led him one step at a time towards the floor safe, slowly stooping down to her knees. He matched his body movements to hers, keeping a firm grip at her nape.

When she flipped the rug up in a quick motion, he jammed the hard object against her neck to remind her of his threat. Zetta placed her thumb on the scan and entered a code.

"WHOOP..WHOOP..WHOOP.. followed by the deafening wail of a klaxon siren startled the man into jumping up, releasing his grip of her shirt. She had entered in a three-digit emergency code instead of the four digits to unlock the safe.

"You Bitch!" yelled the man.

Zetta fell backwards. Untangling her feet from her skirt, Zetta pedaled them on the floor scooting backwards out of the man's reach. She forced her voice not to tremble, "That safe is now on lockdown for fifteen minutes. Security is guaranteed to appear within three to five minutes. Mister, that's just enough time for you to escape without any one getting hurt."

He jerked his head, looking from Zetta to the door and

back again, fury in his posture. Zetta ducked her head instinctively when he swung his arm. The object he flung before running out the door deflected off the table edge, hitting Zetta's bent knee before it clanged to the concrete floor beside her.

♫♪

Thankfully, Poppy arrived soon after them - his touch at work soothing Zetta's agitation.

"First I was plain afraid, then when he shoved that pipe into my neck I thought it was a gun." Zetta swallowed to control the quiver in her voice. She moaned, "I don't know what I was thinking. He could have killed me."

Echo had listened to Zetta repeat her story three times, becoming more incensed with each telling. They watched the images replay on the security video – the quality more grey tone than color due to the reduced lighting.

Disappointed, Echo said, "Other than proof there was an attacker, the video doesn't provide anything significant that could identify your assailant." She tipped her chin at the man in the summer blue uniform shirt taking Zetta's statement and said, "I'll make a copy of this video for you."

"Wait, there is something," Zetta asserted. "He was wearing black pointed boots made out of a skin. Like the ones Bella described that Nash person wore."

The policeman dutifully made a note.

After Moses recounted the events of the past few days, he gave the officer a copy of Nash's photo and the video clip taken earlier that day by Echo, suggesting the police might want to watch out for the white truck.

As the policeman moved to package the pipe and DVD of the security video as evidence, Echo indicated the pipe. "May I?" she asked.

Disconcerted, he handed the plastic bag with the steel pipe to Echo. She opened the bag and dangled her fingers inside without touching the pipe. *Cold nothing. No sense of remorse. Relentless.*

Unnerved by the IF, Echo foretold "We have an implacable hunter. He's going to persist."

Once the door closed behind the officer, Moses declared, "I'll check with Corinne and Maurice tomorrow to see if either of them left the gate unlocked." Accustomed to the Foundation's odd hours, Corrine and Maurice always locked the gate when they were the last to lock up shop. Moses faced Zetta, brooking no argument, "If you insist on going to the theatre tonight, I'll follow you home after. You should be safe with the group during rehearsal. Oh, and you should carry a small can of Raid with you."

Zetta crunched her eyes in confusion. "Raid?"

Moses smiled. "Yep. It's powerful enough to shoot a stream twenty feet away. Aim for the person's face. It burns their eyes as good as mace."

"Zetta, why don't you stay in my guest room for the next couple of days? It couldn't hurt to change up our routine a little to confuse our hunter," said Poppy.

"Even if I have to place a can of roach spray on every windowsill, I'm not going to let some goon scare me out of my own space."

"Then Hawke will lend his photographer eyes to our search of the Preservation Hall archives tomorrow," offered Echo as a way of keeping Zetta inside. "I know you weren't enthusiastic about going with me. Anyway, I sense Hawke's frustration that I'm going to do something rash."

Unh huh," said Zetta, biting her thin lip and staring into space.

24

ST. CHARLES LINE: *only the maker knows*

At the chugga, chugga sound of the engine idling to a stop, Echo joined the small group shuffling into a loose line at the corner of Canal and Carondelet. Coins and transit passes in hand, they waited for the hydraulic door to swoosh open.

Echo selected a seat next to an open window anticipating the leisurely pace of the St. Charles Street Line through the Garden District. The mahogany wooden bench seats, exposed ceiling bulbs and brass fittings, definitely a nostalgic nod to the era in which it was built, added to the charm of the green streetcar.

Immediately after navigating the street car's first turn, a man with briefcase in hand pulled the overhead wire to ring a bell at the front of the car, signaling the motorman to brake at the Lee Circle stop. At this time of day, in the hottest month of the year, more native New Orleanians rode the non air-conditioned car than tourists.

St. Charles Avenue, the Jewel of America's Grand

Avenues, boasts a superb collection of grand mansions among glorious live oak trees. The massive trunks and majestic low spread branches sculpted elegant shade canopies one hundred feet or more in diameter. Only one acorn in ten thousand will grow up to be an oak tree, but these graceful survivors of time were older than many of the prominent families of uptown New Orleans.

The Garden District has twenty mansions, but two hundred fifty shotguns – an architectural thread that ties New Orleans together. Besides the historic Audubon Park, the avenue is residence to the renowned Tulane and Loyola Universities. Echo particularly liked the recently renovated Wedding Cake House with its elaborate cornices, balconies and columns - the embellishments evocative of fondue frosting.

The screech, screech, screech of the iron wheels, combined with a peculiar whirring noise of the electric whip as the car made a ninety degree turn to the right, broke into her contemplation. Echo reached overhead and tugged the wire to signal the conductor.

She ambled along the neutral ground, crossing the street when she located Violet Boudreaux's rose painted house next to the coffee shop.

A boy about ten years old rested his right foot on the porch rail, rocking his chair in short, jerky movements. He looked up from his book when Echo entered the gate. Jumping up out of his chair, he pulled the screen door open and called out loudly into the house, "Mama, someone's here!"

"Li'l Joe, how many times do I have to tell you not to holler?" scolded the woman peering out through the screen. "The colorful scarf twined around her head complemented the attractive woman's glossy brown black coloring. Cocoa colored eyes shifted to her guest, her wide mouth breaking into a welcoming grin when Echo reached the porch steps. "You must be Victoria LaBauve."

"And I assume you're Violet. Thank you for responding so quickly to the note Moses' left for you."

Her left eyebrow arched and with a frank stare at Echo, she said, "To be honest, I was curious. I googled your foundation on the internet but couldn't figure out what you might want to know about my grandmamma."

Echo liked her directness.

Violet waved her over to the open screen door, "Come on in. I hope you don't mind joining me in the kitchen. I'm baking." She wagged her finger at the boy when he moved to follow them inside. "Now, Joe, you sit right back down and finish your book. You're making very good progress."

When his shoulders drooped in disappointment, his mother promised, "We'll have brownies and ice cream tonight to celebrate completing your summer reading assignment."

As Echo followed Violet through the house, she commented, "I remember when I was about Joe's age, my Poppy introduced me to Nancy Drew. I'd curl up on a low branch of an oak tree for hours. It was hard to coax me *away* from books that summer."

Violet's eyebrows twitched and her lips quirked showing she caught the irony. "Well, my goal this summer was to balance my son's virtual world with other activities which might spark his imagination - like reading, Little League baseball, the zoo."

"We'll sit there." She indicated the vintage table in an alcove.

Echo chose a straight backed wooden chair next to the window. Setting her tablet on the pristine white porcelain top, she settled onto a butterscotch yellow cushion and admired the unusual design of the golden oak splats of the chair back - carved in a squat, rounded fleur de lis pattern.

"Here, try my raspberry sun tea." Violet set a glass in front of Echo, then chose a chair next to her. "Beautiful, isn't it?

Mabel brought this table with her when she came to live with us."

"It has such warm character to it," agreed Echo. She and Hawke had kept the old porcelain table in Poppy's cottage, but the craftsmanship of these chairs was spectacularly different yet aesthetically pleasing.

Echo opened the gallery of pics on her tablet then tasted her drink. "Thanks. The clammy heat of the trolley car made me thirsty."

"To quell your curiosity, Violet, my Foundation is helping a neighbor in the Quarter untangle a mystery linked to some items he found when his great-uncle's house was demolished. His great-uncle was Billy Williams."

Victoria nodded her head to indicate she knew the name. "My grandmamma sang with Billy when she was a young girl."

Echo continued, "Someone is obviously alarmed about the discovery. There have been attempts to steal the items, one of my associates was attacked last night and a silly blogging story has people running around looking for treasure."

"One of my quandaries," admitted Echo, "is whether Billy Williams preserved these items to be later discovered and investigated or thought his secret was hidden forever."

Enlarging the photo of the silver cigarette case Echo explained, "Archer found this case with the monogram TMS. Her finger pushed that photo off screen to display the next photograph. "This key was discovered inside of the case. No one knows what the key belongs to, but someone is overly interested in gaining possession of it."

With a light finger tap, the photograph of five people in a club replaced the key. "Your grandmother, Mabel Ball, is in this photograph which Archer found folded inside of the case."

"Oh," exclaimed Violet. "My grandmamma has that same photograph." She walked across the room to a narrow bookshelf and removed two small albums standing among the cookbooks.

"When Mabel came to live with us, I helped her create these memory books from her club days." Violet opened the first album, turned a couple of pages and pointed to an old clipping pressed between the transparent vinyl sheets.

Thrilled about possibly uncovering useful information, Echo asked, "Did Mabel name the people in this photograph? Or ever talk about the significance of the picture?"

Violet cocked her head in reflection. "Grandmamma was eighty-eight years old when she moved back here from Alabama. She relived her music days by telling and retelling the same stories. These two albums represent her most vivid memories."

"This is Billy." Violet pointed to the man holding the trumpet. "When she looked at this picture, Mabel would always say *Sweet Billy - our savior from that devil man.* Then she'd point to this white man." Pursing her lips in amusement, Violet said "But she never gave devil man a name."

Echo showed Violet the clipping of the dead man. "Did Violet ever mention this man?"

Her face twisted into a scowl. "She had a copy of that clipping, too. It always distressed Mabel so I didn't keep it for her memory books. Never understood who he was or why she kept the article. She would whisper, "Billy protect us."

"Billy kept in contact with Mabel over the years. He called her Sister Mabel and it stuck as her stage name." She worked clubs along the Gulf Coast while he became an international traveler. Colorful postcards depicting landmarks from European cities - Stockholm, Vienna, London – appeared as Violet flipped pages in the album.

"May I?" Echo removed one of the postcards from the sleeve, flipping it over to view the back. The message section was blank except for a printed block B.

Violet said, "Mabel said Billy couldn't read or write. He had someone address the postcards for him. That B is his signature."

The dancing sun beams angling through the window cast celery highlights in her eyes while Echo considered what else she could learn from Violet.

"Did Mabel talk about a special key crafted by Billy?"

"No. But she kept that box he made for her. Said Billy joked with her about its beauty being different from any other gift she'd receive."

Violet's face softened at a memory. "Grandmamma would play hide and seek by placing a trinket in the box to entertain Li'l Joe. She would sing something nonsensical when they found the trinket. Something like *We found it, but only the maker can tell us what did he know.*"

Her senses thrumming, Echo switched back to the photograph of the key and asked in rapid fire fashion, "Did the box have a lock? Is it possible this key could fit the lock? Did you keep the box after your grandmother passed away?"

Slightly taken aback by Echo's sudden barrage of questions, Violet's eyes widened. She delivered a hearty laugh, leaning back in her chair. "Grandmamma...."

A buzzer and a wonderful chocolate scent intruded. Violet removed the oblong pan from the oven and placed it on a cooling rack, then turned back to Echo.

"Honey, Grandmamma Mabel is more often confused than lucid nowadays, but she is still alive. She lived with us for five years. My husband, Joe, was a musician. He worked nights and cared for Mabel during the day while I taught. When Joe died suddenly of a heart attack two years ago, I had to find an alternative living arrangement for Mabel. By then she needed a daily caretaker."

The dejected slump of her posture and bowed head conveyed her disquiet with the memory. "I couldn't care for

Mabel alone, yet couldn't afford anything other than the nursing homes which accepted Medicare." Violet's eyes glistened, "I worried that she would think I abandoned her."

"That man writing his memoir rescued us. He told me about the place Mabel now lives in the French Quarter." She breathed a happy sigh, brushing the moisture from her eyes with the tip of her fingers. "Li'l Joe and I bring these memory books when we visit."

Amazed at the revelation, Echo asked, "Does she still have the box?"

Violet tapped the side of her head saying, "Oh yeah I forgot about your other questions." She lifted her fingers to count off her answers. "Mabel still has the box. The box does have a key hole. I never paid attention to it because the box wasn't ever locked and Mabel didn't have a key that I ever saw."

Violet removed a card from the back of the second album and laid it on the table for Echo to read. "Here's the name of the home Mabel lives in. It's run by the Sisters of the Holy Family. You're welcome to visit her. I'm not sure you'll hear anything but the same stories she repeats to us over and over again."

Echo picked up the card. To her astonishment, L'Host Nursing Home was handwritten on the back of a generic business card for Stanton and Silverman.

She machine-gunned more questions at Violet. "Which man gave you this card – Stanton or Silverman? Why was he visiting Mabel?"

Unsure why this was important to Echo, Violet explained it was immediately after her husband died so she didn't pay much attention to his name or looks. The man visited about three times, asking Mabel about memories from the forties – said he was writing a family memoir. She described a stout, medium height man with thinning hair.

Great. That description fit both Stanton and Silverman.

Echo pushed Violet for other memories. "This might be a significant lead in our mystery. Do you remember anything else about him – what he talked about with Mabel?"

Violet leaned her head back against the chair, her brows furrowed in concentration. "When he looked through her collection of stuff, he lingered on some of the programs asking for her memories about people who attended the events. Some of them were fundraisers where politicians and musicians mingled."

"Did he see Mabel's box?" wondered Echo.

"Honey child, Mabel was so proud of that gift she showed it to everyone. On thinking back, he inspected the box closely. He made the mistake of asking Mabel if she knew whether Billy made others like it."

"Mabel was insulted. Told the man that Billy said the box was a one-of-a-kind." With a short spasmodic laugh, she recalled, "She wasn't interested in talking to him anymore that day."

Echo idly flipped through the pictures and notes on her tablet, thinking it was time for her to leave. She would visit Mabel tomorrow.

"Wait." Violet reached across and tapped the image of the cigarette case. "The man wore monograms on his sleeve cuffs. I remember thinking the first time he visited that it was an affectation."

"By his third visit, I had decided he was ostentatious and there's no accounting for bad taste, no matter your station in life. When he crossed his legs, I noticed his socks were monogrammed!" She snickered, "I wouldn't have been surprised if he stamped his initials on his driver's forehead."

25

DOWNTOWN: *empty handed*

He tossed the stack of photos his man grabbed from the Foundation into his desk drawer, slamming it shut. The photos didn't mean anything to him. His father had a copy of the same newspaper clipping about Scarmuzi's death but he was confident there was no evidence left to condemn his family for that murder. He shifted uneasily in his seat, a slight pang of worry. The fact that Billy kept the clipping would cause curiosity. *Would that curiosity drive the do-gooders even harder to find what the key unlocked? That blogger hadn't helped and he wasn't any closer to uncovering Billy's hiding spot.*

If only he knew what that nosy girl thought. Was it true that she could read people? Her grandmother bristled if anyone ever broached the topic. He would make sure he was with his partner whenever he interacted with her.

He stared grimly at his buzzing phone. A text message told him his driver had arrived. Nash's delay was going to make him late for his Tuesday afternoon meeting. He stood up, his heavy stride carrying him into the reception area. His partner's door was closed again. *He was acting strange lately – almost secretive.*

♫♫

He settled into the back seat of the car, his eyes narrowed. "You're late."

Nash grimaced at his boss's chiding tone, "I've been keeping tabs on that snoopy girl, like you told me to."

His voice dripped with cold condescension, "And did you discover anything useful?"

A dim flush crawled up his driver's cheeks. Suppressing an impotent anger, Nash said, "Echo spent some time with the old lady's granddaughter at her house. She was empty handed when she left. She went back to her Foundation office for a short time then I followed her and her Indian husband to Preservation Hall on Bourbon Street. I don't know what they're looking for there and they appeared empty-handed when I followed them back to the Foundation. Anyway, I left them there to pick you up."

The stocky man in the back seat remained silent, chewing on his unlit cigar.

Nash's hands stiffened on the wheel, a muscle pulsed at the side of his neck. He plunged on. "I bet she's going to visit the old lady in the nursing home. Do you want me to suggest to the caretakers that Mabel isn't well enough to receive visitors?"

"Not necessary." The boss rolled the cigar back and forth between his thumb and finger, stubborn arrogance painted his face. "I doubt Echo can unearth anything I haven't already learned from Mabel or Violet. I visit the old lady every couple of months. No change. No new information. She's ninety-four years old and her brain is feeble. She doesn't know or remember anything useful or harmful – just old memories and fear."

"What about that box of hers?"

"What about it? It's empty." Although not spoken, his tone implied *you fool.*

Confused, Nash asked, "So you don't want me to follow her there?"

His boss gave an impatient shrug and heaved a long exasperated sigh. "It's worth watching her, but not because of what Mabel will say. I predict Echo will bring the real articles with her when she visits Mabel." Then with a nasty chuckle, he said, "You'll have an opportunity to recover them."

26

BOURBON STREET: *preservation hall*

Familiar with the Hall, Hawke appreciated the stark simplicity of the shaded room they entered. A piano sat diagonally in one corner. Drums on a worn rug surrounded by mismatched empty chairs formed the Hall's stage area. The size of the room limited the number of listeners who could sit on the long flat cushions, positioned on the floor in rows across from the performance area. Portraits of the musicians who first played the beautiful sounds of New Orleans Jazz lined the otherwise blank plaster walls.

She and Hawke sauntered out the back door of the hall into the courtyard in search of a volunteer. Eager to share his knowledge, the portly man they met in the alley way escorted them to an old carriage house beyond the courtyard and up an exterior staircase.

He informed them this was not an official archive. "We've built quite a nice library with volunteers collecting and organizing printed and recorded materials. Many of these items were rescued from garage and estate sales." He unlocked the door revealing floor-to-ceiling shelves covering three walls of the long, narrow windowless room. Echo shivered from the frigid temperature.

Discouraged, Echo dropped into one of the chairs next to a small round table in the center of the room. *Oh my God. Were those accounting ledgers?* Overwhelmed by the numerous rows of green binders, she asked the volunteer, "How do you find anything in here?"

He puffed his chest out, "I'm proud to say I helped organize the room. No one does handwritten accounting entries any more. Someone donated these old ledgers after they moved all their financial records to computer." He pulled one of the burlap green covered binders off the shelf to demonstrate. "We converted the ledgers to albums. Paper sheets were specially cut and drilled to fit these adjustable posts."

Returning the book to the shelf, he indicated the rows. "We have a few albums dedicated to famous musicians – like Louis Armstrong and Jelly Roll Morton, but most of our material is organized by timeline. The books on this wall are organized by year. The earliest records we have date back to 1930, but our material is pretty sparse between 1930 and 1935."

"We'd like to browse 1939 and the early forties," said Hawke.

"Sir, wait." The man pinched his lips, agitated by Hawke reaching for a ledger, "Is there something specific I can help you locate?"

Hawke instinctively understood the man's reluctance to have strangers handling delicate, aged paper. "To be honest with you, we don't know what we're looking for, but I promise you we'll handle these with extreme care."

The man stood, undecided.

Everybody loves a mystery. Well, maybe everyone except

Grandmother Esme.

Echo held up her tablet displaying the clipping of the five people. In an attempt to entice the volunteer through curiosity, she said, "We'd like to know what else was happening on the Jazz scene around the time this photograph was taken. It was published in a March 1939 Sunday newspaper spread about Jazz musicians." She tapped the man dressed in a suit seated in the picture. "And we're trying to identify this man."

The volunteer's eyes glistened at the challenge. He relented. "You'll need to wear these." He slipped his hands into thin white gloves and handed matching pairs to Hawke and Echo before moving to the row of 1939 ledgers. "How can I help?"

Echo quickly listed their assignments. "Search for other pictures with the same interior as this photograph." With a sideways glance at Hawke she said, "If we can identify the club, Zetta can trace ownership. Hawke, you focus on our dead guy. That leaves me surfing the contents until something flashes."

She used her tablet to photograph several programs, news clippings and photographs, tagging those which aroused curiosity, suspicion or instinct.

Satisfied they might have found some helpful threads of information; Echo removed her gloves and thanked the volunteer, leaving him to put his archives back in order.

They exited the hall onto the corner of Bourbon and St. Peter. Echo dug her sunglasses out of her bag. Her eyes watered from the shock of the glaring sun after being cooped up in a windowless room for a couple of hours. They followed St. Peter Street southeast to Royal, holding hands.

Hawke allowed her a few minutes of introspection, then rubbed the palm of her hand with his finger to get her attention. "Did you flash on anything?" he asked.

"Hhmm?" she murmured distractedly.

He tickled her palm again to return her attention to his question.

She answered with a sigh, "Nothing acute. More like misfiring sparks. Maybe when I review what we collected, something will bubble to the surface."

They stopped outside of the courtyard gates. Hawke faced her, his eyes compelling and magnetic. "I know you're anxious to start. I'll leave you with Zetta to conjugate your thoughts." He kissed her goodbye and headed home to his workshop, troubled that her sparks would trigger reckless behavior.

Preoccupied with their own thoughts, neither noticed they had been followed.

♪♪

Accustomed to Echo's manner of organizing her thoughts, Zetta waited in her reclined gaming chair while Echo pushed and swiped photographs on the large wall screen. Once she was satisfied, Echo brushed a curl off her face and settled into one of the purple suede chairs.

"We found these pics in one of the 1939 ledgers. Notice how the interior in these four pictures are very similar to the photo found by Archer? Someone had written club names on the album page but there's no guarantee they are accurate. The Open Door and the Twenty-Five Club."

Zetta squirmed with anticipation of the hunt. She said, "Hey, those are two of the clubs mentioned in that montage article. Tax assessor records are probably the best source, but they are recorded by address. I'll have to trace backwards from current club addresses until I find these old club names. Then maybe we can get the owner's identity."

Controlling the screen from her tablet Echo showed the

next two images. A Christmas program, titled *A Winter Jazz Holiday*, featured the Blue Keys, a Jazz quartet with a blues soloist. 'Local Politicians and Oil Executives Celebrate at Annual Petroleum Club Event' headlined the photograph next to the program. The caption under the photograph listed the names of people in the photograph.

"This is Luciano Scarmuzzi, our dead man." Echo drew a circle around a man who stood off to the side of the group in the background. The caption says this guy at the front table is Marcel DioGuardi. Isn't that the mobster family that was big back then?"

She drummed her fingers on the arm of her chair. "I wonder if Scarmuzzi's protection business was associated with DioGuardi? And if so, what does that tell us?"

"There was a feature in the Arts and Leisure section of the newspaper about a fundraiser in February 1940 for the newly rebuilt Charity Hospital. In addition to shots of the Jazz musicians, there was this." She enlarged the next photograph. Three rows of men and women dressed in formal suits and gowns smiled into the camera. A man, center front row, proudly held up a mock check. Attendees boasted titles of attorney, politician, oil company representative, property owner and doctor.

"Read the names." Echo instructed Zetta, zooming in on the caption.

Zetta scanned the list, uttering the names. "Wow, it sure is a small world. You blue bloods really stick together." She pointed to the man holding the check. "Thomas Montgomery Stanton. Is this Teddy's grandfather or uncle? He looks old.

"According to Grandmother Esme, that is Teddy's father's name."

Vittoria Bertucci. Is he any relation to Sal? Tilden Martin Silverman II." Zetta paused on the third row. "And is that your great-grandfather, Arthur Delahaye, standing next to him?"

"Well, hail, hail the gang's all here." Zetta sang with faint amusement. "But we still have two candidates for our mysterious TMS."

"Here's my last curiosity." Echo swiped the screen. They looked at a snapshot from an April 1940 newspaper with the caption 'Members of the City Planning Commission celebrate.'

"Billy Williams is one of the musicians on stage in the background but that's not what caught my attention. The main focus of the photograph is this group," she said pointing to four men at a table. "Stanton and DioGuardi. City Councilmen and a known Mafia guy are drinking together."

Tapping a spot on the picture, Echo said, "And this looks like Scarmuzzi at the table in the left corner. This was taken the week before he was shot."

Zetta inhaled a deep breath and whistled.

27

Chartres Street: *bird man*

The golf umbrella sheltered her upper body from the short, intense thunderstorm. Plump drops fell steady and fast, plopping into puddles, spattering onto her long yellow cotton skirt. *The skirt had seemed like a good idea in this muggy, sticky heat.* The grey low-hanging clouds appeared to be parked long-term – in contradiction to the weather forecast of a brief, light rain.

Her feet squished in open sandals, as she walked past St Mary's Italian Church, adjoining the old Ursuline Convent. Built in 1752, the Convent is the only remaining French-colonial building in the United States. The original convent, school and gardens covered several French Quarter blocks.

Echo admired the simple white concrete façade of the buildings which had served many purposes throughout its history including a makeshift hospital and orphanage, but now housed the Catholic Diocese archives. Concrete benches surrounded by clean formal lines of shrubbery invited one to rest their body and mind. Behind the main building the restored herb gardens, a favored spot of Poppy's for its extensive selection, flourished in the rear yard of the Old Convent. One of the nuns, Sister Xavier, in essence became the first pharmacist in the United States, compounding medicines. The teas, infusions and distillates she brewed from the herbs in her garden represented the greater part of what was available in those days for treatment of the sick.

Zetta's research revealed the home Sister Mabel lived in further up Chartres Street was converted from a small hotel and managed by a different order of nuns. The home appeared to be surviving on charity, government grants and private contributions. Even then, Echo didn't understand how Mabel's granddaughter could afford this place. *Was Mabel's care unknowingly being subsidized?*

Of particular interest to Echo was the fact that Stanton and Silverman owned the property. As Zetta would say *A coincidence, I think not.*

She leaned against the brick wall under the partial eave to escape the rain, closed her umbrella and shook off the excess moisture before entering the thick oak door.

"Oh, how vintage," exclaimed Echo. A tree mural done in brown, grey and black tones dominated one of the pastel blue walls. What impressed Echo was the absence of a chemical smell which usually assaulted you in nursing homes. The only obvious sign of the hotel's conversion to a residential nursing facility was the aged residents sitting on a green vinyl chrome legged couch and in wheel chairs clustered around a 1950's boomerang style coffee table.

Inquisitive eyes followed Echo across the well worn parquet lobby floor. The old feeling of being an outsider nibbled at her as she approached the young woman in nurse scrubs sitting on a stool behind the original guest reception counter.

"I'm here to see Mabel Roche." Echo handed her card to the nurse. "Her granddaughter should have called ahead to clear my visit."

The nurse smiled. "We're always happy for our guests to receive visitors." She hesitated, "I'm not sure how much she'll talk with you, though. Sister Mabel is having an off day today."

"Off day?" asked Echo.

"Most days she's interactive, engaging in some form of conversation. Today isn't one of her more coherent days," she said, leading Echo through a hallway entrance next to the reception desk. "Come this way. I'll show you to her room. Whether cogent or not, the performer in her still enjoys an audience," she said kindly.

The regal posture of the light black-skinned woman with cropped silver hair belied her ninety-four years. With the exclusion of the hospital bed, the bedroom was a throwback to the fifties, furnished with a chest, dressing table and chairs in light blonde wood. Garbed in a blue dress with pink pearl buttons, her feet clad in laced support shoes, Mabel sat in a straight backed chair facing away from the door. She watched Echo enter the room through a reflection in the round mirror of the dressing table.

"Miss Mabel, you have company. Someone who knows your granddaughter, Violet," said the nurse, inviting Echo into the room.

Pulling a second chair closer, Echo sat. "Miss Mabel, my name is Echo LaBauve. Violet showed me your memory books and shared some memories with me. I was hoping you'd talk with me."

Mabel cocked her head slightly and mumbled what sounded like "unh hunh."

"Do you remember singing with Billy Williams?"

Mabel's lips moved. Echo leaned in close to listen. It sounded like she whispered, "Billy no more."

Echo removed the newspaper clipping from her purse, showing Mabel the picture of the musicians in the club. "This is you with Billy. Do you remember this?"

The placid expression on her face neither confirmed nor denied her recognition.

Pointing to the suited man sitting at the table, Echo asked "Do you remember this white man?"

The old woman crossed her arms protectively across her bosom, closed her eyes and started humming, rocking her head from side to side. "ummumm, nnn hmm. ummumm, nnn hmm"

Oh-oh, not the reaction she was hoping for. Concerned she had upset Mabel, Echo looked around the room for a way to distract her. *Oh my, that looked like the box Billy made for her!*

Touching Mabel's shoulder softly to get her attention, Echo pointed to the box on the chest. "That's a beautiful box. May I hold it?" Mabel continued her humming, but slowed her rocking motion, her eyes focused on Echo's movement.

Echo carefully handled the box. Again trying to engage Mabel, she asked, "Didn't Billy make this for you?"

Mabel started to sing, her voice crusty and wobbly, "Billy, hey Billy, sweeeet Billy. Oh oh yeahhh."

Beautiful with its dark and light woods fitted together like a complex puzzle, the box lid opened easily on its hinges. Stored inside were a gold cross on a fine chain and a flower brooch made of colored glass. *No clues there.*

An intricate three petal silver design encircled a keyhole, but the design obviously didn't match the silver key. Its opening laid horizontal rather than the typical vertical placement. And although there was a keyhole, there was no latching mechanism to lock the lid to the box. Intrigued, Echo turned the box searching for hidden cavities. The box appeared to be exactly what it purported to be – a pretty wooden gift made especially for a friend.

Discouraged, she thought, "*Darn. I had high hopes for the key fitting this box or Mabel remembering something significant.*"

Echo held the box close, rubbing her hands over the warm wood before replacing the box on the chest. No flashes. *If only she could conjure up IFs on demand.* She returned to sit with Mabel and silently placed the cigarette case and key on the dressing table watching for Mabel's reaction.

Mabel ignored the key, but stretched her hand towards the tarnished case, her long tapered finger tracing the monogram. "The old suit man," she said, her words clearly enunciated.

Continuing to trace the monogram trancelike, Mabel sang in a bluesy tone, "Open dat door. Suit Man, oh de Suit Man. Him don't hurt us no more. Ohhh no no nnoo...."

Mabel stopped singing. Her head drooped forward with her eyes closed. She sat silent. After a while, when Echo thought the old lady had dozed off, she quietly stood to leave. Mabel didn't seem to recognize the key. *Maybe she didn't know anything about what Billy had hidden.* On impulse, Echo slipped the cord around her neck thinking it really did made a pretty amulet.

She picked up the case, dropping it back into her purse. IF! *Mabel still feared the old man in the suit who this case belonged to. How was that possible?*

She thanked the nurse on her way out and waved goodbye to the residents. They happily waved back. *Nope. Not an outsider unless I want to be,* she thought, retrieving her oversize umbrella from the antique coat rack and umbrella stand in the lobby. Outside, the intense rain storm from earlier morning had tapered to sheets of lumpy clouds hiccupping fat raindrops.

Echo wondered how Mabel could still fear the man in the suit. More than likely he was dead. Did she believe, in her confused moments, that he was still alive? She tapped a message into her phone while balancing the umbrella tube in the crook between her shoulder and neck. A swishing sound grew louder behind her. Echo started to move aside to avoid the muddy splash from bicycle tires rolling through puddles. The swishing tempo speeded up.

In the next instant, she recalled her dream of a bird landing on her shoulder. Alert to menace, she turned the large umbrella sideways, using the ribbed covering as a shield. A large booted foot kicked out, catching the umbrella ribs before landing a glancing blow to the back of Echo's shoulder. She sprawled onto the sidewalk; her phone snapped open into three pieces as it flew out of her hand striking the concrete. She shifted her weight, rising up to her knees. A man in a camouflage poncho jumped off the bike, yanked her purse off her shoulder and shoved her hard. Echo grabbed the tip of her umbrella swinging the shepherd's hook handle sideways to trip the man when he lifted his leg to re-mount the bike seat. He stumbled, the bike wobbled, but he didn't fall.

Swinging around, he planted his combat style boot in the middle of Echo's back keeping her from seeing his face. Echo felt something cold and hard press against her neck. The man leaned in. In a harsh tone louder than a whisper, the camouflaged man said, "Stay down Witch!" He climbed awkwardly back on the bike. Maybe the tip of her umbrella bruised his leg.

She lifted her head in time to see the man pedaling away. Tied to the handlebars, Abraham's red and yellow parrot, Scarlet, flapped her wings, jumping up and down in the basket, squawking ""Awkk. Down witch. Awkk."

Echo jumped up and ran down the street, shouting, trying to get anyone's attention, "HELP! Someone stop that man!"

Other than the man and bird on a bike, the street was deserted. She saw no one else out in the rain.

"Awkk. Help! Awkk. Stop!" mimicked Scarlet. The bird's screeching didn't slow the fleeing cyclist.

♪♪

"Only the custodian from the old convent witnessed anything helpful," said Moses. He squatted next to where Echo sat on the curb, her crippled umbrella shielding her from the drizzling rain. "He confirms the man and bike but the poncho hood hid the man's face. He says he didn't notice a bird. He was more concerned about whether you were hurt."

Annoyance washed over Echo's face.

Moses hesitated. What he said next would peeve her even more. "I don't think our local constable believes you're a reliable witness, Princess."

The policeman reached in his rain slicker to return his notebook to a uniform pocket then headed back to his motorcycle parked near them. Lifting his helmet from the seat he said to Echo, "I've finished speaking to the few people who ventured out onto the street when they heard you shouting. No one saw anything that can identify the thief."

Exasperated, Echo huffed, "Officer, I told you this is more than a purse snatcher. I believe this guy had a gun. And I already told you, I can identify him from his scent." She had recognized the smell of Nash's cologne when he bent over her neck.

The young motorcycle cop rolled his eyes, with no pretense at believing in a woman's intuition.

Hawke, observing the fire in his wife's eyes, arched his eyebrow at Moses and tipped his head towards the policeman. His unspoken message, *Take care of this before Echo's temper flares and she says something rash.*

Moses, the peacemaker, stood and clasped the young man's shoulder with his left hand while shaking his right hand. "Thank you, Officer. I understand how far-fetched some of this may sound to you; but if you check, you will find that another report was filed Monday night for a similar attack on another Foundation associate. We believe the same person is responsible."

He kept his body language loose, but hardened his voice to preacher mode, "It might behoove you and other officers of this fine city to be on the watch out for a white truck with illegally tinted windows. Should you encounter the truck, you might want to check the occupant for weapons."

As the young officer rode off on his motorcycle, he laughed to himself. *"That was one stunning, but delusional woman. Pretty crazy story - a talking parrot on a bike with a gunman in a poncho who she can identify by smelling him. And it's not even the weekend. Maybe it's a full moon."*

When Moses' tablet computer pinged an incoming video call, he stood next to Hawke and Echo so they could all view Zetta on his mobile screen. "Yo, girl genius. Status?"

Stark black round frames emphasized the serious glint in Zetta's eyes. The background changed as Zetta paced back and forth. "Ok. Echo, your passwords are all changed and your tablet is locked so whoever took your purse will not be able to access our server or breach our security. I'll have a new tablet configured and ready for you by the time you get back here.

Moses frowned, "Is the GPS on her tablet still active?"

"Yes sir." Zetta responded facetiously. "It's tracking beacon is sitting still --- drum roll, please -- in the same block that Stanton and Silverman offices are located. Are we going to try to get the cigarette case and key back?"

Echo's snicker drew their attention. In answer to their questioning expressions, she pulled the cord from inside her shirt exposing the key. "Mr. Cologne Man may have the cigarette case, but we still have the key. I don't think his boss is going to be happy."

"Well, I guess that's one for the foresight side of the

Foundation's balance sheet," smiled Zetta.

Hawke pointed to Echo's torn, muddy skirt. "Why don't I take our street urchin home to change clothes before she meets you both back at the Foundation?" The scowl on his face belied his light tone.

♫♪

She selected a cranberry dress with short cap sleeves made of t-shirt jersey fabric, wincing at the tightened skin from her abrasions.

He watched his wife tame the explosion of curls, fingers nimbly braiding her hair away from her face. Looking at her as if photographing her with his eyes, he considered her composure a stormy serenity - incongruous as that may seem.

Echo caught his shadowed eyes watching her in the full length mirror. She stuck her tongue out at him trying to lighten the mood, imagining he was brooding about her safety.

There was an inherent strength in his face. Hawke cupped her face gently between his hands, gazing into her turbulent green eyes. His voice, like warm flannel, "You had a very prescient moment today, Victoria, and I know you managed to take care of yourself before me" his thumb stroked her bottom lip, "but for the rest of today let me be your partner."

She grasped his hand and kissed the palm. She dropped her hands, still holding his, in a pose of tranquility. Tipping her head back, she gazed into his eyes. "I know it may be hard for you to believe that I wasn't being impulsive. I sensed his menace, but didn't intuit that he really meant to use the gun - just frighten me. Besides in my dream, he only landed on my shoulder." *Oops, that didn't come out right.*

Gentleness and patience evaporated from Hawke's posture. "Unbelievable. You knew you were going to be attacked?"

Her passive act wasn't erasing the stern displeasure on his face. Not wanting to dwell on the gun, she said, "Ok," she relented. "He's a mean ignoble man and I need to take his desperation into consideration when next we tango."

Feeling his posture stiffen, Echo hurriedly clarified, "I meant tango in an academic sense – battle of intellects. I promise you I don't plan to physically wrestle with anyone over a key."

Not willing to give in to her wiles just yet, he said, "That's the problem, Victoria. You never *plan*. You just spontaneously entangle yourself in dangerous situations."

She gazed up at him, silently beseeching his forbearance. The intense color of her eyes could be mesmerizing when her emotion overflowed.

Hawke wrapped his arms around her, hugging his wife tight to his chest. His mouth curved in tolerance, he murmured in a self-deprecating humor, "Just remember some people are more immune to your bewitching than I am."

♪♪

They walked together in silence, each lost in their own sentiment. A fine mist rose from the small pools of water scattered on the street and sidewalk. Choppy abstract patterns of light danced on the buildings from the afternoon sun which beat its way through gaps in the clouds. The heat of the fractured rays evaporated puddles quickly, releasing water vapor into the air. Humidity - one adversary Echo couldn't outsmart. She patted her head, attempting to tuck the escaping curls back into her braid. Leaving the sun to jockey with orphan raindrops, she and Hawke entered the sanctuary of her Foundation.

♪♪

"Your new tablet is completely formatted and secure. I downloaded all the notes, photographs, etc for Archer's mystery." Her clipped speech and restless pacing troubled Echo. Surprisingly, Zetta appeared unfazed yesterday after her wrangle with the intruder on Monday night, but her edgy behavior today surpassed her norm. *Was this a delayed reaction?*

"I had scanned the pics and clipping before bobble head stole them Monday night, so they're included in there. Now they know we are interested in the dead guy. We don't know why Billy kept that clipping." Hands on her hips, Zetta stopped in front of Hawke who was scrolling through the notes on Echo's replacement tablet. "But they now know we will be considering it a clue. If we identify Scarmuzi's connection, will that tell us who is behind this ridiculous key chase?"

"How much caffeine have you had today? Drink this," Echo instructed Zetta, pointing to the steaming clear brown liquid. "It will smooth out those jitters."

Zetta wrinkled her nose at the mug of tea Echo placed on the kitchen bar. "Ugh," she grunted, but slumped onto a bar stool and sipped the potion.

Echo crossed her arms on the counter and leaned forward, forcing Zetta to look directly at her. "Zetta, what happened the other night can be paralyzing and intimidating. I feel guilty and responsible for placing you in jeopardy. If you are frightened by what happened today after your experience Monday night – want to take some time off or work safely from home, I'll understand."

"Afraid?! Listen, Echo, that's not what's wrong with me," Zetta's voice rose to a sharp pitch. She pressed her small hands together in a praying gesture. "What's wrong with me is that I'm NOT scared. I'm seething."

"The crud who jerked me around and kicked you is mean, but he's disorganized and careless. Whoever his boss is, he's foolish to depend on this guy." Twirling her glasses, she said, "We can outthink them. We need to figure out who the boss man is."

"Apparently, Victoria, you are not the only female with a malfunctioning fear gene," interjected Hawke.

His sarcastic humor ruffled. Echo swung into her warrior stance but before she could argue the observation, the front door swung open with force. Moses rubbed his cropped hair to shake the wetness out, ignoring his damp khaki shorts and guayabera shirt which he favored.

"This amateur is pretending to be Abraham." Moses' hard voice pumped out his discoveries. "Abraham's bike and Scarlet were abandoned a few blocks past the cathedral. Abraham said someone stole them while he was in a bathroom. I'm not sure if he was more agitated over the theft or that the thief left Indigo behind - loose on the sidewalk."

Zetta looked across the counter at Echo with a mock grimace of pain. "Did I mention that the jerk is also stupid?"

Echo whistled two short bleeps. Everyone stopped talking. *Poppy taught her that. And, of course, Grandmother abhorred the behavior - unbefitting.*

She waved her hand at Moses, noticing a couple of fingernails were broken. *Ugh, going to need a manicure.* "Start with the GPS signal and follow any suspicious activity by Stanton – or Silverman. Do your Ranger thing."

He frowned and teased, "I'd have to shoot them, then."

"Ok. Ok," said Echo in mock dismissal. "Do your PI thing instead."

Contrite about implying earlier that Zetta was intimidated or fearful, Echo hugged Zetta and said, "I recorded the diddy Mabel sang. The phrase *open dat door* sounds nonsensical but probably isn't. Focus your property search on the Open Door Club. See if you can link Scarmuzzi, the suit man, to the club in any significant way."

Echo looped her bag over her shoulder and added, "Just don't chase any cowboys or spacemen without me. Lock the door and arm the security when you are alone in here."

"And keep your Raid ready," added Moses.

"Where're you going?" asked Zetta, Hawke and Moses in unison.

Their earlier conversation still fresh in her mind, Echo said with emphasis, "Hawke volunteered to be my partner for the rest of today. He's going to help me find a dress for the gala." Indicating her scraped knees and elbow, she said impishly, "I don't have anything in my closet that will hide these from Esme."

Hawke groaned. "Can we at least go to one of those places with soft armchairs that serve drinks to attentive, indulgent husbands?"

Her expression changed from playful to serious. Echo rubbed the amulet between her fingers. "They've discovered by now that they don't have the key."

Careful not to muss her braid, Hawke lifted the cord over her head transferring it to his own neck. With a sly smile, he said, "Meanwhile, let's play musical chairs with the amulet."

Echo recollected one of her dreams. *Was this what the hot potato game meant?*

28

ROYAL STREET: *louisiana scandals*

F-a-r-c-e. Double word score twenty, plus eight for extending the word ant to ante. *Darn. She missed her personal goal by two points.* Echo flipped the token red side up and turned to Sal who stared out his store window, the ever present unlit cigar chomped between his teeth.

"I heard about your mugger yesterday. You ok, girl?" Sal asked.

Echo appreciated that he didn't mollycoddle her but the term, mugger, made her grimace. "It wasn't a purse snatching, but the police don't believe me. Whoever jumped me snatched my purse to get the case and key."

Continuing to stare out his window, he made a tsking noise, "Archer should've never had his picture taken with them for the newspaper. I told Bella nothing good was going to come out of it. Are you going to stop digging into the past?" he asked.

Echo crossed her arms, jutted her fine-boned chin out

and demonstrated how obstinate she could be. "No, Sal, I'm not. I don't believe Billy ever meant for his secret to be revealed, but we can't ignore that three people have been assaulted." She persisted, "Whoever wants the key is already riled up and I know he will not stop hunting for it."

He stood in the same slouch since she arrived staring silently out the window, rolling his cigar round and round between his thumb and forefinger, lost in thought.

Attempting to lighten his mood, she showed Sal the Charity Hospital fundraiser group photo. "Look what I found in one of the albums at the Preservation archives. That's my great-grandfather, Arthur. And here's a Vittorio Bertucci. Could you be related to him?"

Sal glanced at the man who glowered into the camera. "He's my uncle. In fact, I inherited this store from him." He sounded almost melancholy. "Vittorio headed the Merchant's Association back then during a very difficult time for immigrant small business owners."

He rubbed his thumb repeatedly across his index and middle fingers in the universal sign of money and said, "He was bitter. Had to contend with the Mob and corrupt politicians. Used to say sometimes you couldn't tell them apart. I'm glad times have changed."

Echo changed the subject again. "Are you and Bella attending the fundraiser tonight?"

"Yeah. Officially, we represent the Quarter Merchants Association." He finally grinned. "In truth, we go because Bella looks forward to the glamour of the night. She's out right now getting her hair done." He pointed his cigar at her, a slight smile lighting his face. "And me, I go to make her happy."

♪♪

Zetta descended the stairs from the loft. Tiny bright

colored clips pulled her short hair back into vertical rows away from her round face. "So you've dropped Sal from your list.

"Yes. We just learned from Moses that he believes our intruder had a key to the courtyard gate. Stanton and Silverman own this property."

"Seems obvious it must be one of them families. So we remain all eyes on Stanton and Silverman," said Zetta.

"Who will both be at the gala tonight," Echo said from where she lay pensive in the gaming chair.

"As will be your Grandmother Esme," Zetta reminded her.

"Uh-huh. I just need to figure out the right questions to ask without creating a ruckus."

Zetta snickered. She picked up her remote from the chair arm and carried it to the couch with her. She squirmed back into the cushions, paused, then slumped far enough to set her small feet on the driftwood table. Satisfied she had found a comfortable position, she said, "So I don't know the original owner of the Open Door yet. Still working on a trace. It's more tedious than I anticipated. Too bad there isn't a directory of people listing all the properties they own. You have to start with the property."

She moved into a sing-song delivery. "We've been tracing the *who* is worried about a secret, but I've been wondering about *why* there is a secret. The clipping found in the cigarette case is dated March 1939. The newspaper with the dead man is a year later in April of 1940."

Zetta flicked a button on the remote to display a timeline with a list of headlines. "Let's view it from the perspective of Billy's time."

In 1939, the country was recovering from the Great Depression and moving into World War II. In contradiction to the rest of the country during the Depression, the quality of life in Louisiana was on the upswing because millions of federal dollars were funneled to this state. However, much of that money was pocketed by public officials and businessmen in a wave of corruption known as the Louisiana Scandals. Public figures frequently helped themselves to public monies and properties. During a five year period after Huey P Long's assassination in 1935 there were grand jury sessions, charges, denials, investigations, indictments and verdicts. Hundreds of people were implicated in wrongdoing and some were indicted. Distinguished citizens went to jail. The architect who designed Charity Hospital was one of those convicted.

DioGuardi had established an illegal gambling empire with the help of political officials. He bought bars, ran a liquor store and gobbled up real estate. He had become the head of the New Orleans Mafia.

Politics before Governor Long in Louisiana was a dirty business dominated by influence peddling and cronyism. During Long's tenure in the thirties, he mastered a patronage system and re-shifted the tax burden from the poor to the wealthy class, large corporations and utilities. He taxed oil operators provoking their wrath. The oil-and-gas industry came to Central Louisiana in a big way with the discovery of the Olla Field in LaSalle Parish.

Zetta pointed to the screen. "Big Brush Charlie's perception about the gangster fedora might be real. I found a spider web of relationships in which our dead man and our two prime suspects were connected to the New Orleans Mafia Boss. DioGuardi sat on the Railroad Commission with Tilden Martin Silverman the second. He amassed real estate holdings as did Stanton and Silverman. Stanton and DioGuardi appeared together in photographs with members of the Mineral Board and City Planning Commission."

"So both family's wealth and holdings grew during that time period," concluded Echo.

"Yes." Zetta displayed an article published in February

1940 which announced Pennant Oil would build a petrochemical plant next to its refinery. The plant was to make rubber, aviation fuel, and gasoline, which were in high demand for the war. Stanton supported the plant, boasting it would employ ten thousand people.

"What's interesting is the reporter opined that Stanton's support was self-serving being that he owned over six hundred acres of oil rich land. Stanton Jr. has since sold most of the land. He only kept ten acres with a cabin for hunting and fishing."

29

DOWNTOWN: *the blue room*

They yellow cab stopped in front of the brass plate sign on Baronne Street, close enough for the doorman in his gold-buttoned dark olive green uniform to assist Hawke and Echo out of the taxi, without blocking the view through the grand revolving door. Originally The Grunewald Hotel, the Roosevelt Hotel was renamed for President Teddy Roosevelt in 1928. Its massive, ornate lobby with glittering Italian chandeliers, mosaic floors and coffered ceilings stretched an entire city block with a duplicate revolving door exiting onto University Place. The hotel had been restored after Katrina to its grandest era of the 1920's and 1930's.

"Good evening. Welcome to the Roosevelt. May I assist you?" The doorman's pleasant, bland smile suggested he had been repeating the greeting often tonight.

Hawke returned his smile, showing their embossed invitations. "We're attending the fundraising gala in the Blue Room. It's just inside this door to the right, I believe."

"Yes sir. Someone is managing admission just inside the lobby past the clock." In deference to their evening dress, the doorman held open a heavy glass door allowing them to bypass the turnstile entrance. "Please enjoy your evening."

Hawke and Echo paused inside the wide, long lobby to admire an imposing conical pendulum clock which stood nearly 10 feet tall. Atop the white and brown marble base, a bronze sculpture of a robed female held a scepter adding grandeur to the old time piece. The scepter moved in a constant circular motion near the black onyx clock face, rotating soundlessly from the female subject's hand.

Hawke escorted Echo into the Blue Room - the one venue that continually drew the stars of stage and screen for unforgettable performances at the height of the supper club era in the early 1930's. During its heyday, from the thirties to the sixties, countless households tuned their radios each Saturday night to await the announcement, "We're live, from the Blue Room," as the house orchestra began performing with a flurry of horns.

"If these walls could only speak, the stories they'd tell," Hawke said, in appreciation. They entered the storied space, decorated in deep blue and rich gold. "So many celebs performed on stage over the years when this was a swank supper club - Louis Armstrong, Ella Fitzgerald, Frank Sinatra, Jimmy Durante, Marlene Dietrich. Later on - Ray Charles, even Sonny & Cher and Bette Midler."

"It's now relegated mostly to wedding receptions and fundraising events." Echo squeezed her husband's hand. "Sad, but I guess the romance and intimacy of the sixties isn't profitable enough."

Alicia Silverman waved to get their attention, weaving her way between the crisp white-clothed round dinner tables to greet them. "Oh, Echo, what a simply scrumptious dress. Honey, that copper color is the perfect complement to your incomparable hair and eyes."

Reminiscent of a more refined and elegant time in fashion, the shimmery satin, full-length, backless evening dress draped fluidly over Echo's body. The hairdresser had persuaded her to forego her usual chignon, styling her ginger hair instead in long sophisticated waves which framed her classic oval face.

"I arranged for you to sit at the table sponsored by Stanton and Silverman." Alicia said with pride. She pointed to a table set for ten people at the right center of the dining area.

The horns section of the orchestra heralded the next big band number in keeping with the entertainment theme of the gala - the Audubon Swing. Unlike the mood of the Great Depression, the music of the thirties was upbeat, jazzy, and happy.

"Thank you, Alicia. We look forward to visiting more with you at dinner." Dark and handsome in a single breasted, short-jacket black tux, he had tied his hair back, the short tail tightly bound in an ebony leather thong. Hawke rested his hand low on Echo's back, guiding her towards the section of the spacious room where the silent auction was being held.

He placed his mouth close to her ear and in a husky velvet whisper, said with banked passion, "So tempting. I'm looking forward to my reward for helping you find this dress."

Halting a short distance before reaching Esme, Hawke turned Echo slightly towards him. "I'm not foolish enough to believe you will let your mystery rest for tonight given that we know someone from Stanton & Silverman's office is involved." He gently tipped her chin up, gazing into her exotic green eyes accentuated by smoky taupe liner. "But, Nancy Drew, can you provoke in moderation?"

Echo opened her mouth to deny any intentions to goad Stanton or Silverman, but then shrugged her shoulders in capitulation. "Ok, I'll try," she agreed.

She hesitated when Hawke quirked his eyebrow as if to say *really*. "Truly," she said in response to his expression. With a coquettish twinkle in her vivid eyes, she looked at him and vowed, "Tonight I am Victoria LaBauve, poster child for the Delahaye School of Etiquette and Protocol."

Hawke shook his head, his thin upper lip barely breaking into a smile. "Come on, minx, let's mingle. I'll feast on this view," he said trailing his strong fingers down her bare back, "while you mesmerize others into divulging information."

They joined the small group surrounding Esme and waited until she completed her sales pitch. "The hot items for auction this year are these autographed jerseys from the football and basketball teams. Fortunately for our fundraising, there's strong competition among the bidders." Esme turned away from the group, leaving the couples to strategize about their bids for the coveted jerseys.

The straight nickel grey dress, its bodice beaded in silver and puce, was a classic design which suited Esme's cool blonde beauty. She hugged her granddaughter and Hawke then scrutinized Echo. "Victoria, you look so elegant tonight."

Inferring that normally she didn't?

"Well you can thank Hawke for his impeccable taste in dresses," Echo said with a slight curtsy.

"Alicia has assigned us all to her table. I'm afraid her interest in the Foundation may wander beyond its community programs." Esme winced, wrinkling her forehead into scowl which Echo was dreadfully familiar with. "Victoria, I realize this may perplex you, but I'd appreciate your appeasing her curiosity about your mystery work."

Huh? What alien had taken over her grandmother's body?

Esme clarified further. "With restraint. We mustn't monopolize the table conversation."

And there's the royal We. Really? I'm twenty-nine, not nine.

Hawke stroked her back, quieting the dragons in her

head. "We don't want to keep you from your hosting duties, Esme. Victoria and I will see you later at dinner."

How did Hawke find it so easy to be Mr. Manners?

His fingers tapped against her spine, signaling for her to move towards the bar.

Echo sputtered, "With restraint?"

Hawke threw back his head, a laugh rippling in the air, the amusement in his eyes infectious. Echo couldn't control her burst of laughter. "You heard her. I have her blessing to talk about my mystery – as long as I *restrain* myself."

Her gleaming eyes sobered, "Uh-oh. I haven't been awfully successful at the restraint part. And I'm sure she wouldn't approve of me meditating during dinner."

Hawke chuckled, raised his wine glass in a toast, caressing her with his dark caramel eyes. "You can appease me later tonight and no restraint necessary."

"I hope I'm not intruding." Martin Silverman signaled the bartender for refills from where he stood behind Hawke.

He reached over to shake Echo's hand. "We were introduced after the Jazz Mass. Alicia is a fan of yours and especially excited that you and your husband will be joining our table tonight."

Echo introduced him to Hawke after which Silverman pulled in the slender, fit man sporting a mustache and rimless glasses who stood at his side. "This is Professor Clark. He's advising me on the harsh realities of a state campaign."

"Professor." Hawke tipped his glass in a gesture acknowledging the introduction. "Do you teach or have you abandoned academia for politics?"

"I consult on campaigns in addition to teaching Masters level political science. My specialty area is economic and community development. Even though he's the one who's been courted to run for state office, Martin, here, is being diligent."

"Whew," said Martin. "There's a lot to withstand from

public opinion. Voters judge candidates by personal characteristics as much as they do for where the candidate stands on issues. Experience, honesty, morality, compassion, competence, leadership."

"Ahh! Could that be the anxiety I sensed in you last Sunday?" Echo trained her face into a nonchalant expression, but watched closely for Martin's reaction.

Martin spluttered, took a swallow from his drink, and with a humorous gleam in his eye, wagged his finger at the white streak in her waves. "My wife warned me about your ESP. Although I want to understand the rigors of a political campaign, young lady, I'm not anxious about it. You probably sensed me brooding over some business deal with my partner."

He gulped another swallow from his drink. "Stanton is impulsive and I'm methodical. I'm nineteen years younger than him. Makes for a rocky partnership sometimes especially when we represent different viewpoints." His tone hinted at discontent. "Our own personalities are much like our fathers. I often marvel how this family partnership persevered sixty-seven years.

He reached out and touched Echo's hand. "See, I'm calm."

FLASH – Cyan blue. Physically calm.

Echo set her wineglass down, taking his hand gently between her own, hoping to experience a more in-depth flash. *Confident he will be untainted.*

Intriguing. Untainted by what?

"Yes," she assured him. "Extremely calm and confident."

With a clash of symbols, the band played the opening stanza of The Trolley Song - *Clang, clang, clang went the trolley. Ding, ding, ding went the bell.* Leaning her pretty blonde head towards the microphone, Alicia Silverman invited everyone to find their assigned seats so dinner could be served.

As they made their way across the room, Echo lowered

her voice to share her IF with Hawke.

♪♪

One of their table companions commented on the hotel's history as host to presidents, royalty, movie stars, musicians and athletes.

"Our own Huey P. Long kept a suite at the Roosevelt which he used as his headquarters in New Orleans." said the Professor. "He reportedly stored his deduct box in a safe in his suite."

"Deduct box?" asked Alicia.

"One of the legends revolving around Governor Long." said the professor, "Every state employee who received a job from Long was expected to pay between five and ten percent of his salary to Long's political machine. Those funds were kept in the locked deduct box"

"Estimated at more than $1 million annually," The professor's wife, a history teacher, added. "The deduct box has never been found after Long's death but a replica is displayed in the lobby."

Her fair face alight with transparent curiosity, Alicia exclaimed. "Echo, wouldn't it be exciting if your mystery key opened up something like the deduct box?"

Teddy Stanton leaned his thickset body back into his chair drumming his fingers on his chest. With a derisive smile he pinned his small eyes, their pupils contracted under straight blunt eyebrows, on Echo. "Tell us, Ms. LaBauve. Do you believe the key Archer discovered leads to a treasure?"

Out of the corner of her eye, Echo noticed Grandmother Esme's face stiffen but she couldn't stop what popped out of her mouth.

"Treasure? I think that's illogical. Billy wasn't wealthy. Why would he hoard something with value? Seems reasonable if there was treasure that could be spent, he would have spent it on himself or family, or even to help others."

Martin sipped his wine, an inquisitive look on his face. He asked, "I have to admit curiosity about the combination of items found by Billy's great-nephew. What's their significance to each other? Have you constructed a theory about them?"

Measuring her response, Echo said, "I think Billy kept something hidden – information, a secret, evidence – something only he and maybe someone else in the photo knew about and that he never intended to reveal it. Maybe the cigarette case is not connected. Maybe it's a trinket Billy picked up from one of the clubs he played in."

She waved her newly manicured index finger between Teddy and Martin. "Coincidentally, two people at this table have initials which match the TMS inscription. That same monogram could adorn either of your family silver."

Esme gasped.

Alicia's tinkling laugh broke the tension. "Oh honey. Not the Silverman's. Martin's family silver is inscribed with a single S."

The history teacher asked, eagerness in her voice as she let herself be caught up in the story, "What do you plan to do with the key?"

"Now there's a conundrum. Archer doesn't know what the key belongs to and doesn't have any reason to care." Echo said with a wry grin and an expectant expression. "One option is to let whoever keeps trying to steal it have the key. But then will that person continue invading Archer's life in the belief that he also has whatever the key belongs to - which by the way, he doesn't?"

"Another option is to throw the key in the river or melt it to eliminate the risk of exposing whatever Billy secreted away," interjected Hawke.

Echo agreed, a reluctant shadow in her eyes, "Probably

the best solution, but a pity to destroy such exquisite workmanship."

"Excuse me, folks, I have to return an important phone call." Stanton stood. "I apologize for the interruption."

The professor excused himself, too, moving in the direction of the lobby.

The strained look on Grandmother Esme's face – as so often in the past - cued Echo. She changed the subject to the Saints football team's winning streak.

♪♪

"Stop." Hawke hissed, tugging her back away from the front stoop of their home. He indicated the illumination between the louvers of the plantation shutters in the front window. A movement disrupted the slats of light.

"Wait here." He edged close to the window. Tensed for action, he peered through the slats.

"What the hell," he exclaimed, "is Moses and Poppy doing here at this time?" He relaxed his stance, waving Echo over.

30

HOME: *duct taped*

Moses paced while he explained. "We agreed I would escort her home after rehearsal. When I didn't hear from her by ten-thirty, I called her mobile. No answer – so I drove over to the theatre and found her Vespa still parked outside."

He had arrived to find a darkened stage. Zetta's fellow actors were packing up their gear to leave. No one remembered her saying goodbye. Moses walked around the immediate vicinity without finding any hint to where she may have gone. Her satchel, which a fellow actor found resting on an empty seat during their search of the back and side stage areas, lay on the floor at Moses' feet. Her phone, tablet and keys were in the satchel. Wherever Zetta was, she was without her personal communication devices.

"Urgent mail, I see." Yoda's light saber glowed red, awakening Echo's tablet.

Too worried to interact in Yoda-speak, Echo touched the icon for the Foundation's general email. A red exclamation point marked an email from *thecatandfiddle*. The subject line shouted in caps, URGENT YOU READ.

Moses asked, "What does the child blogger think is so important?"

A few seconds later, they discovered he had forwarded an email with no subject line. The sender, using *thefixer* alias had written just two terse lines of instruction.

Find the treasure. We'll trade your girl for the book.

Echo shook her head in confusion. "What book?"

"We need to get this to the police, but in the meantime let's try to scare up some more info." Moses' square shaped fingers slowly typed out a message. He held out the tablet for everyone to see before he hit send. *Not until I speak to Zetta.*

The email finally chimed, ending several minutes of silence. Delivered from the same alias. When Echo played the attached video clip, they watched in astonishment. An immobile Zetta sat up against the headboard of a bed. A bandage wrapped across her eyes and around her head. Her ankles were bound loosely with rope. Duct tape wound tightly around her upper body fixing her upper arms to her sides while allowing some movement of her hands.

"This is my fault," said a distressed Echo.

Her phone rang, caller ID blocked. Hawke pushed the speakerphone answer icon and started the record mode.

"You got proof. Now get started." The caller spoke in a low nasty growl.

Angry at herself and angrier at the persons responsible for abducting Zetta, Echo stubbornly shot back – her words like a bullet coated in crunchy peanut butter. "No. Not until I speak with her to make sure she's ok."

Her heart raced at the responding silence.

"Hello, Echo?" It was Zetta.

"Zetta!"

"I'm ok. I'm ok."

"You're injured. Your head is bandaged." Echo was babbling.

Zetta sounded exasperated when she said, "*IF* you would only listen to me, Echo." Zetta paused. "They just used the gauze to blindfold me. My eyes and ears are just fine."

"Thank God," uttered Echo with a shaky sigh of relief.

In a flat, but calm tone Zetta continued to say, "Would you please check on Mr. Earl for me tomorrow? Since it looks like I'm going to camp out in the company of these peoples in their home, would you ask Moses to cancel my visit to the bobble head theatre? I was so looking forward to that first sweet smell and hearing the red and blue ornithology orchestra."

"That's enough," the caller growled. "Mrs. LaBauve, the sooner you turn over the book, the sooner this smart-mouthed girl can go home."

"But what book?" asked Echo. Too late. The caller had already hung up.

Horrified that the caller had disconnected the call, Echo rambled. "We need to do something. She sounded upset with me. What did she mean if only I would listen to her? We can't just leave Zetta out there."

Hawke held her hand, rhythmically rubbing his thumb in circles on the inside of her wrist until she quieted.

"She was reconciled. She recognized the potential volatility of her situation, but was confident that she wasn't in imminent danger." Poppy interjected, his voice and demeanor like balm to a bee sting.

His mesmeric blue eyes rested on each of them in turn garnering their attention. "More importantly, I believe our Zetta was giving you clues. Her lemon yellow aura means she was giving us strong direction."

Poppy rose and stood behind Echo, resting his hands on her shoulders – using his *touch* to focus her. He saw what others couldn't. The violet aura at the crown of Echo's head revealed she was idealistic and highly intuitive. Brilliant spots of white light glowed at the palms of her upturned hands. His granddaughter was exceptionally gifted and cause-oriented.

"Shă, I think she was telling you to use your intuition. When she said *If only you would listen,* she placed more emphasis on IF."

"*IF,*" he repeated. "Isn't that her mnemonic for your talent?" With a slight smile he said, "I believe she calls them intuitive flashes."

They replayed the recording, listening with intent to what Zetta said.

"Ok. The first is easy," said Echo. "She wants me to check the computer searches she has running. But are they significant to solving some part of the mystery or finding her?" worried Echo.

Poppy pointed out, "Zetta addressed different items to you and Moses. If we trust our girl genius, she is divvying up duties to run simultaneously. You, Echo, focus on solving the mystery or finding the treasure. Let's assume she's giving Moses hints to find her."

"Remember, she referred to her attacker the other night as a bobble head," said Hawke "so I think she's indicating he's the same person who now has her tied up."

Moses asked, "Ornithology orchestra. Is she telling us that she can hear birds? How does she know they are red and blue birds if she's blindfolded?"

"Scarlet and Indigo," Echo and Poppy said in unison.

"The obvious, I guess." Shrugging her shoulders, Echo said, "She heard them speak."

"That leaves her most obscure reference *camping with these peoples,*" said Moses.

Hawke broke in, "It's two o'clock in the morning. I think everyone needs to rest for a couple of hours."

"We can't abandon Zetta," Echo disagreed, in disbelief that anyone would or could sleep while Zetta was in danger.

Shaking his head emphatically, Hawke spoke authoritatively to override Echo's stubbornness, "Moses will take this to the police. We," he said circling his finger to include Echo, Poppy and himself, "can't accomplish much more in these dead hours after midnight. We can sketch our plan of action in the morning when we all have fresher views."

Poppy sympathized with his granddaughter's impatient eagerness to take action, but agreed with Hawke. He coaxed Echo. "Just four hours rest, Shă. Time enough for your subconscious to speak." He reassured everyone, "This guy isn't going to harm Zetta as long as he's depending on you to find something very important for him.

31

UPTOWN: *motivation*

"Not to worry. I'm holding her genius girl in a good location. That redheaded witch now has an incentive not to melt the key and to find the treasure. But, Mr. S, it didn't sound like she knew anything about a book."

"I don't give a damn whether she knows about the book or not. I want the nosy bitch motivated to find where it's hidden."

Nash, believing he had figured out all angles, boasted, "If she doesn't know about a book and can't find it, your black gold is protected. We can negotiate the smart aleck's return for the key."

The man regretted hiring the idiot. He planned to make sure the Italian knew how dissatisfied he was with his referral.

He growled into the phone, "Just stay in touch. Only use the phone I gave you. Don't screw this up if you value your own life."

"No worries. I'm taking care of it."

Zetta stiffened at the sound of footsteps returning, convinced her kidnapper was Nash. She had overheard his side of the conversation. If only he had spoken the other person's name. Was Mr. S. Stanton or Silverman?

32

The Foundation: *in a blink*

Hawke turned with anticipation towards the oriental, spicy fragrance only to find an empty pillow wore the sultry perfume of his wife. The digital numbers on the bedside clock showed five o'clock. Sitting up on the edge of the bed, he rolled his head on his shoulders a few times to clear the grogginess of a short sleep.

His bare feet whispered across the floor to the balcony where he found Echo curled up on the settee. "Couldn't sleep?" He sat next to her, drawing her close into the warm strength of his arms.

"More like half-sleep. Closer to lucid dreaming than slumber. Don't worry. I've tamed my manic emotion from last night," she said, her eyes on fire, "and now I'm ready to start our hunt."

♪♪

They arrived at the Foundation office before dawn, a time when even this city appeared to slumber.

Hawke turned the sound effects off on the computer. He didn't want to disturb Echo while he read through Zetta's research and notes from the past week. Zetta must have expected them to find something specific. After the first hour of dwelling on the meanings of Zetta's message, Echo dozed off on the couch while Hawke checked Mr. Earl.

A gauzy sheet draped over a line. A wind blew in, whipping the corners sharply. With each flap, the sheet blurted. "IF. IF. IF."

The sheet blew away in a gust of wind, a hazy pathway emerged, the smooth mellow notes of a trumpet calling to her.

She walked down the path, looking right, looking left.

The seductive sound of the instrument pleaded with her to stay on the path. Unafraid, her heart pounded in anticipation as she followed the horn player, merely a shadow, along the twists and turns. A dim protective hue enveloped the shadow.

"Wait, please." She said in a hoarse whisper.

The horn beckoned her further like the pied piper.

"Can't you tell me where we're going?" she called out.

The shadow rested in front of a row of dwarf size oil rigs with keyholes all cast in the same mold – that of a fleur de lis. He blew a fanfare before putting his trumpet away. He snapped the case closed and said with a soft quietude, "Why, back to the beginning, of course."

The lock on the Foundation's door double clicked as it disengaged. The aroma of hot donuts announced the arrival of Moses and Poppy and disrupted Echo's dream.

"I couldn't resist. Kim's light was flashing and I needed a sugar high," Moses called out. He flipped open the lid of the white cardboard box. "Hot from The District. Glazed or apple fritter."

Kim, an immigrant Chinese, converted a defunct fast food building on a corner near the police station into a bakery shop with a drive-through window. His business thrived even though he had built it based on an ingenuous belief of a stereotype characterization in television and movies – that donuts qualified as one of the primary dietary groups for policemen. Employing a tradition from the fifties, he added a blinking light outside to announce hot donuts or French bread. Kim opted for a red light to symbolize good fortune. Soon after, in a display of infantile humor, a rookie cop dubbed Kim's Bakery 'The District' referring to New Orleans's historical legalized red light area which had been nicknamed *Storyville* after the alderman who set up prostitutes for the district.

"I need some caffeine to go with that sugar," called Echo in a froggy voice. She rose from her supine position on the leather couch.

Poppy pushed a mug of steaming tea across the counter towards Echo when she and Hawke joined them at the bar. "A special brew to fire the neurons in your brain. What about you Moses?" He explained in an aside to Hawke and Echo, "Moses hasn't slept since he left us last night."

"Thanks, but I'll stick with my espresso, Rouge." Moses placed his cup under the spout of the coffee brewer.

By the time he drank two espressos and scarfed down an apple fritter and a couple of glazed donuts, Moses caught them up on the hours he had spent at the Eighth District Police Department on Royal Street.

It took him twenty minutes to convince the front desk clerk he wasn't delusional or a kook, then he had to wait another ten minutes after the shift change to be assigned to a grizzly detective whose bored expression changed quickly when Moses reported Zetta's kidnap. Skeptical about motive, and disbelieving that an old key would drive felony behavior, the detective spent the first hour grilling Moses as if he were a suspect.

Frustrated by the waste of time, Moses reminded the

detective he was with Echo when she received the video and persuaded him to consider the police reports of the break-in and assault attempts filed by Archer, Zetta and Echo. Finally, the police posted a BOLO on Larry Nash and the white truck suspected of belonging to him.

Moses concluded his story. "I showered and changed, discovered you two gone, picked up Poppy and after our detour for sustenance, here we are. So, have you thought of anything new?"

"Well, Echo brooded over Zetta's message then fell asleep." Hawke looked deeply into Echo's eyes. "So what have you intuited?"

"I was deconstructing what she said, not brooding." Echo took a deep breath, exhaled and said, "I'm so worried about her that I don't know if I'm overanalyzing – reading more than there really is in her words."

Poppy touched her hand, "Let's hear what you think. We'll be your sense check."

"She said her eyes and ears were fine. Did she want to assure me she wasn't hurt? Or did she really mean she could hear and see through the gauze?"

Hawke's raised eyebrow and Moses pinched mouth intimated they doubted her assessment.

"And I dreamed about a gauze sheet harping at me."

Poppy encouraged her. "And if so, how is that significant?"

"Because that lends new meaning to her other statement. Listen." Echo replayed the recording from last night.

Since it looks like I'm going to camp out in the company of these peoples in their home...

"The whole phrasing of this sentence is awkward and not how Zetta normally speaks. She says camp, not camping. Company. Peoples is plural. Home, singular."

Echo rubbed her eyes with the heels of her hand. Taking

another deep breath, she spouted what she knew was a stretch of imagination. "What if she could see that she was on Camp Street? And she's trying to tell us she's being kept in a home with many persons run by a company."

Poppy mused, "Nursing home, group home, boarding house."

"Possible." Moses said. "Someone's done an amateurish job implicating Abraham, who I hear lives in a boarding house."

"That someone is Nash." Intransigent, Echo insisted, "The bit about *first sweet smell* is Zetta's way of telling us Mr. Cologne Man kidnapped her."

Moses relented. "Probably. What have you found?" he nodded his head in Hawke's direction.

Hawke summarized, "The results of Zetta's information searches point to Stanton."

"The Stanton family is the original owner and operator of the Open Door. The Seniors Stanton and Silverman created a partnership in 1945 incorporating some of their individual commercial properties into joint business holdings. The Open Door property is part of the partnership's combined holdings, but the Juniors have nothing to do with the operation of the Jazz club which now leases the building. Stanton Senior's property ownership increased significantly in the two years leading up to the 1940 scandals. Even though Stanton Junior sold most of the land, the family has considerable income from oil revenue. Their mineral estate is dominant over any surface rights."

Hawke commented, "Could be the Stantons were involved in illegal activities but escaped investigation during the scandals."

"And does the key lead to proof?" asked Echo, fingering the pendant around her neck.

"Ok. We search and discover in pairs." Moses tweaked

Poppy's pony tail. "Poppy and I are on our way to find a boarding house. I assume you'll concentrate on finding something the key unlocks."

Right after Moses and Poppy left, Echo sighed, "What have I missed? Surely Billy wouldn't have hidden a key without there still being a lock it fits. Mabel's box is the most obvious, but this key doesn't fit that keyhole."

Hawke motioned for Echo to sit on the couch facing the wall screen and said, "Victoria, you're blessed with enhanced intuitive insight which means you process visuals, words, expressions incredibly faster than the average person – in a blink. Let's experiment with that."

"While you dozed, I created a slide show of pictures, headlines and highlighted notes from the investigative file pulled together by Zetta. Just relax and watch. If there's something recessed in your thoughts, it will pop for you."

Echo rested her head back on the couch's cushion, her eyes attentive to the shifting images on the wall screen. IF! When the monitor darkened, she remained silent, dwelling in her imaginative thoughts. After a few minutes, she bounced off the couch and beckoned Hawke to follow.

"Let's start hunting."

"Where?"

"Back to the beginning."

33

UPTOWN: *ragged people*

Poppy went into the Museum Store while Moses waited in his Jeep parked at the curb. He shook his head side to side when he exited on his way next door. A few short minutes later, Poppy climbed back into the idling car. "Both Archer and Sal said Abraham lives in a boarding house on the other side of Canal, but neither know the address."

Moses dialed the number of a VA counselor he had worked with on another case. His call concluded, he said, "She was willing to help, but the address they have on file for Abraham's disability checks is a post office box which isn't going to help us."

They trolled the Quarter with Moses chauffeuring Poppy from spot to spot searching. Too early for much tourist activity, they didn't find Abraham working. Poppy spoke with a tarot card reader outside of Jackson Square where Abraham sometimes entertained with his McCaws.

"She says Abraham lives in a home somewhere upriver

on Camp."

The sun beat down on the windshield as they rolled up and down Camp Street identifying three obvious signs of boarding houses. The first house included a lobby and manager who didn't know Abraham. The tenant responding to Moses' knock at the second house declined to invite him inside and claimed not to know Abraham.

"This isn't promising," uttered Moses. He parked in front of the third house on their list. A woman with purple streaked hair answered his knock and shook her head no when asked if Abraham resided there. The home catered to women, not men.

He slumped back into the driver's seat pinching the bridge of his nose. Frustrated, Moses grabbed his phone and searched the internet for boarding houses. He skipped over the multiple listings for Bed and Breakfast and Guest Houses, found the three houses they had already visited listed under Rooming and Boarding Houses, continuing to scroll through the search results. Clicking on a link, he showed Poppy an article about a property owner complaining about illegal boarding houses operating without the proper license.

"Isn't that interesting," he said.

Poppy swung the Jeep door open and marched up the sidewalk back to the front door of the last house. The same young woman responded to his knock. When asked about illegal boarding houses, she nodded in assent and directed him further up the street.

"Old white house on the right corner, two blocks up." Poppy climbed back into the car, directing Moses further up Camp Street.

Moses eased his foot on the brake, slowing the car as they passed the tired looking house, its faded white paint peeling like week-old sunburned skin. He turned onto the side street, circling the block. Tall windows overlooked the porch and balcony which wrapped around the side and back. Naked two-by-fours patched the broken handrail of wooden stairs which climbed from the back porch to the balcony. An old Buick Roadmaster sat in the crushed clam shell driveway at the back of the property, its back passenger door a brown junk yard replacement mismatched to the original blue metallic of the car. A three-wheel bike with flags, two motorcycles and various bicycles crowded the shallow back yard between the porch and driveway. Parked on the back porch at the top of a ramp, an older gentleman in a plaid shirt and house slippers sat, smoking on a mobility scooter.

Moses parked out of sight of the house on the backside of the block so he and Poppy could strategize. They decided Poppy would be the most unobtrusive, agreeing he would visit the inside of the house for reconnaissance. He looked Poppy over. The old man's demeanor and dress - favorite tattered mesh shoes mended with silver tape and chino pants shabby from so many washings - would raise no suspicions.

At the thought of the men who called this unlicensed boarding house home, Moses recalled lyrics from Simon and Garfunkel's song, 'The Boxer'. *Laying low, seeking out the poorer quarters.. Where the ragged people go.. Looking for the places only they would know.* He hummed a line to himself *Still a man hears what he wants to hear and disregards the rest.* Yes, Rouge would blend right in with the boarders.

Poppy called Moses' phone then slipped his own into his shirt pocket, keeping the line open so Moses could listen in while he was in the house. From where he stood across the side street near the back property line, Moses had a good view of the side and back of the house. He pumped his fist when someone confirmed Abraham lived there and directed Poppy upstairs, listening to the conversation that followed.

"Good day, Abraham."

"Hey there, Rouge. What're you doing here?" asked

Abraham.

"Looking for a friend. How come you're sitting in a chair in the hallway and not your room?"

"A guy staying here is paying me to watch his room. He had to go get a doctor for his sick girl friend. Wanted to make sure no one disturbed her."

"Maybe I could help her." Poppy reached towards the doorknob.

"No!"

Moses tensed for action when a chair scraped against the wall and crashed.

"He said he's paying me because he knows I'll follow instructions." Abraham sounded agitated. "No one can go in there in case she's contagious."

"Did you see his girlfriend?"

"No, man. I told you. She's probably contagious." Abraham's body twitched, too skittish to sit.

"You're doing a good job, Abraham." Poppy said soothing him. "I'm going to keep looking for my friend." He uprighted the chair. "Go ahead and relax back in your seat. I'll see you later."

He walked at a crawling pace along the hallway, watching to see if anyone else showed an interest in the exchange between him and Abraham. On impulse, he exited the door at the end of the hall. As he suspected, it brought him out to the back balcony where the smoker sat on his scooter.

♫♫

Poppy rejoined Moses at his surveillance point. "Upstairs, street side, third door from the right." He pointed to the front of the balcony. "Based on the space between the doors in the hallway, each room probably has one window so that third window should be the room Abraham is babysitting."

Waiting until the man drove his scooter indoors, Moses climbed the back stairs. He sneaked along the empty side balcony, peeking into windows. There! He spotted Zetta through tears in the lace curtains. She sat bolt upright, her upper body now taped to an ancient upholstered chair. *This guy really likes his duct tape.* Nash had left the television on, tuned to the discovery channel with the volume loud enough for Moses to hear the program through the closed window. In addition to the blindfold, the goon had wrapped the gauze, wedging it tightly between Zetta's lips to gag her.

The window didn't budge when he tried raising the lower sash. He inspected the top of the sash and found it locked. Relieved that Zetta appeared unharmed, Moses backed away.

"I can break a pane and unlock the latch to get inside," he said to Poppy when he returned to their observation post. "If we can rescue Zetta through the window without disturbing Abraham, we stay ahead of Nash."

Poppy said, "I can distract Abraham while you get Zetta out."

"Old Man, Echo would not thank me if you got caught in the house." Moses pointed to an abandoned washing machine. "You'll stay behind there where you have a clear view of the front corner, side and back of the house. The TV is on loud enough that Abraham shouldn't hear me. But use that loud whistle of yours if you need to warn us."

Moses halted Poppy when he started to move. "Let's check in first before we crash this party." Moses dialed Hawke's phone.

34

French Quarter: *a fat lily*

Jerome and his buggy rolled past fueled by the mule's undulating gait. A carrot dangled from the tip of the whip which Jerome had extended just beyond the equine's white muzzle. He spoke to the mule, "You're doing good, Mr. Butler. That's it. Steady plod. Steady plod."

Sounds, colors and movement magnified and shivered around her. Echo increased her pace, her body tensed in anticipation. She and Hawke hurried down Royal.

"You ok?" asked Hawke attuned to her edginess.

"This walk feels interminable." Echo shrugged her shoulders. "I'm worried about Zetta. And I don't have any other ideas beside my flash on the trumpet case."

"Finally." They arrived at the Museum Shop.

Archer turned towards the rush of warm air through the open door. His eyes rounded in surprise when Echo and Hawke entered his store. Archer shook his dreads out of his face and blurted, "Man, I'm so sorry about Zetta. This would never have happened if I didn't get you mixed up in this."

Impatient to test her theory, Echo waved her hand to shush him. "We got ourselves involved. Archer, I need to see your uncle's trumpet case again."

Puzzled, he opened his mouth to speak, but Echo interrupted him, quelling her urge to scream. "Now. Please."

Echo bounced from one foot to the other waiting for Archer to remove the instrument from the display box. He placed an oblong wood case battered from years of travel and use on the counter top and moved aside, allowing Echo to inspect it. The case lid had a simple swing latch to hold it shut. No key necessary.

Echo directed her questioning eyes at Archer. "Did your uncle build this case?"

Startled by the idea, Archer stuttered, "I. I, um, don't know. My Daddy never mentioned it."

Echo lifted the brass trumpet from where it lay nestled in the blue velvet interior blocked to fit the bell and valves of the instrument. She pulled on a tab which lifted a raised portion of the interior revealing a tiny bottle of valve oil long dried out, a polish cloth spotted with grey from shining the instrument and an extra mouthpiece. Echo removed the items and ran her hand across the worn velvet until she felt an irregular grain in the cloth. She picked at that spot sliding her fingernail into a slice in the fabric and lifted a small flap of velvet divulging a hidden keyhole.

"I'll be darned," exclaimed Archer.

Hawke removed the key from around his neck where he had transferred it before leaving the Foundation and handed it to Echo. When she fitted the key into the slot and turned, the blocked form for the trumpet bell sprung up and open.

The secret compartment disclosed a sheet of paper and another fleur de lis pendant threaded on a cheap beaded chain. The unlined sheet of pink stationery contained a note written in a childish, loopy penmanship.

Mr. Scarmuzi was shot and kilt in aallie behind the open door. We didnt kill him but we know who did. We didnt touch no gun nor his wallet and watch. We took the silver case and notebook as evdince. The book is hid to protek ourselves.

Signed Mabel Ball and B.

Dated April 27, 1940.

The pendant, a stylized lily woven into a fat, squatty design with rounded petals lay flat in her palm - the flower petals rendered into three distinct appendages.

"It's silver or maybe pewter like the key."

Hawke's phone rang with an incoming call from Moses. After learning they had found Zetta, he told Moses what they had at that moment discovered.

Two seconds later, Echo's phone buzzed with a text message from a blocked number. *Time running out. Did you find it?*

Confident that Moses and Poppy would rescue Zetta, Echo ignored the kidnapper's message.

35

CAMP STREET: *to the rescue*

Moses tapped the butt of his gun hard enough against the top pane to crack the glass, knocking away the jagged edges. He reached his hand through the opening, unlocked the window, and pushed up on the sash. *Damn, stuck.* Curling his fingers to form a short flat fist, he tapped the base of his palm along the window edges. He crouched and put all his weight into shoving up on the window until he broke the aged paint seal. He stepped into the dingy room. Zetta cocked her head towards the noise, mumbling behind her gag. She strained against the duck tape.

Zetta froze at the sound of his pocket knife flicking open. Moses unwound the gauze from her eyes first. He put his finger to his mouth, pointing to the door to indicate they must remain quiet. When Zetta nodded her head that she understood, he cut away her gag and the duct tape tying her to the chair. He pulled her out of the chair and waved towards the window.

She looked back and forth around the room, not moving. He whispered, "What?"

"I need my shoes and glasses," Zetta said in a hushed voice.

He rolled his eyes at her feet clad in orange socks with purple and red stars. "Leave them," he hissed. Carrying her over the broken glass, he pushed her through the open window.

With Moses following close behind her, she tiptoed along the upper balcony, sighing in relief when they started down the stairs.

A shrill whistle caught their attention. Poppy pointed behind Moses calling out, "Hurry."

Moses grabbed Zetta around the waist and scrambled down the steps two at a time when they heard the balcony door crash open. When Nash leaned over the balcony rail waving a gun, he pulled Zetta, zigzagging across the backyard towards the old Buick. A shot shattered the driver's door window.

Zetta screamed and froze. Moses yanked her arm and kept running until she was safely behind the large hunk of metal. "Stay right here. Don't move away from this tire unless I tell you to," he ordered.

A second shot sounded like it hit the washing machine. Moses called to Poppy. "Rouge, you ok over there?"

Poppy replied with a quick double whistle.

Zetta punched Moses in the arm and yelled at him, "Why don't you shoot him?"

Moses didn't want to turn this into a gunfight or hurt anyone. He shouted. "We know who you are Nash. Call off the hunt."

The thin man sneered and called back. "Man, it's too late for that."

Even if anyone cared enough to report the gunshots the likelihood is law enforcement wouldn't arrive for another twenty minutes. Moses wanted to give Nash an incentive to leave. "Echo found what the key opens. Tell your boss there was no book – just an old note. If you leave now, you might escape the police."

Silence rained as if someone had flipped a switch. No birds tweeting. No dogs barking.

Poppy whistled. "Here he comes."

Moses heard the rumbling of a motorcycle muffler and scooted with Zetta behind the Buick's trunk, out of sight, just as the bike revved past on the side street. He pushed Zetta's head down and ducked when he spotted Nash's arm swing out. The Buick's front tire whooshed flat. The fired shot missed its mark a third time. After all sounds of the motorbike engine disappeared, they rose from their crouched positions behind their metal guardians.

"Let's get you back to safety. I'll call that grizzly detective assigned to this and he can take care of the patrol cops when they decide to show up." Moses marshaled Zetta and Poppy to the car, snapping Zetta's seatbelt on after she settled into the backseat.

He glanced in the rearview mirror as he leaned forward to turn the key in the ignition. Zetta crossed her legs and sat stiff and still.

"You ok?" He asked in a gruff voice.

A blush crawled up her neck spreading onto her face and she squirmed. Sounding like a cat trussed up in a corset, she said, "Could we find a bathroom real quick? I really have to pee."

Poppy laughed. "Me too, Shă."

Moses drove three blocks, turned right on St. Charles and pulled into a coffee shop parking lot. He reported to the detective first then called Hawke while he waited in the car for Poppy and Zetta.

36

French Quarter: *begin again*

"Mabel wrote and signed this note. We need to talk with her again. See if she remembers anything."

She twisted the squat lily pendant, studying it from different perspectives – rotated in a circle, upside down, sideways. Blue violet glowed in her mind. *Honor. Inspiration.*

Echo mused, "Your Uncle Billy was a complex man. He created a scavenger hunt with riddles."

FLASH! Mabel's box has a three point filigree design framing a keyhole which resembles the shape of this pendant.

Stirred up by her fevered imagination, she said, "This is Billy's way of looking at life through the wrong end of a telescope. This pendant could be a key in disguise. Let's look at Mabel's box again to see if there is a hidden compartment."

Out on the sidewalk again, Hawke directed Echo further up Royal to Dumaine Street, breaking off their walk when they reached their public garage. "We'll drive instead of walk," said Hawke.

♫♫

Hawke edged the three cylinder auto out the garage entrance towards Chartres. A half-block past the L'Host Nursing Home, he backed the midget car into a short space between two parked cars, parking perpendicular to the curb.

She pushed through the front door to meet empty silence. No nurse at the front desk. The empty space around the boomerang table and aroma of baked chicken suggested the residents were at lunch.

"This way," she whispered to Hawke, following the hallway she remembered from her first visit. She wasn't sure why she felt the need to speak softly. She eased the door open to Mabel's room.

Mabel turned her cropped silver head away from the window where she stood holding onto the tall back of a chair. "Hello girl. You come to visit me again. Who the handsome man you brought wit you?"

Did Mabel really remember her? Was she alert enough today to have a sensible conversation?

They caught a fleeting coquettish smile before the old woman dipped her head.

"I'm Hawke." He sauntered across the room to offer Mabel his hand. In a gallant fashion he motioned to the chair she stood next to. "Would you like to sit here and visit with Victoria and me?"

Her bony finger pointed at Echo, she said "You liked my box."

"Yes. I think your box is incredibly special. Would you show it to Hawke? He's an artist like Billy."

Cautious not to upset her, Echo retrieved the box from the top of the chest and placed it in Mabel's lap.

Mabel's hand shook, fretting over the box lid as she sang, "*You found it, but only the maker can tell us what did he know.*" She raised the box and handed it to Hawke. "See how pretty?"

Admiring the craftsmanship of the golden oak and mahogany wood pieces fitted together like a jigsaw into the shape of a box, he examined the filigreed keyhole closely. He passed the box to Echo with a slight assenting nod.

She cast an anxious glance at Mabel before inserting the fleur de lis pendant into the keyhole. It fit. And turned. The key kept turning freely without triggering any unlocking mechanism. Echo tested the key again and again for any hint of movement, touching every jigsaw piece at the turn of the key only to be disappointed. Baffled, she set the box aside and removed the note from her bag.

When Echo showed Mabel the sheet of pink stationery, the old lady shuddered, crossing her long thin arms in a protective self hug. The alertness in her eyes dulled in reaction to Echo asking if she remembered the note.

"Mabel, can you tell us who Billy was protecting you from? Who shot Mr. Scarmuzi?"

The questions disturbed her. She hummed, rocking back and forth.

Echo said to Hawke, "I wish I had Poppy's ability to soothe. My senses are so fired up, if I touch her right now, I will only agitate her more."

Hawke leaned over, hugged Mabel and rocked with her until she calmed. "Billy kept you safe, Mabel. We'll keep you safe, too. No one will hurt you now."

She uncrossed her arms and tapped the pink note in a metronome motion. *Old suitman aimed for his heart. Old suitman we didn't report. His open door, but the old suitman a menace no more.*

Mabel raised her chin, her brown eyes cleared. "Girl, you come back and visit Sister Mabel again, you hear? You, too, Master Hawke."

♫♪

"Her suit man is not the same as the man in the suit in your picture," Hawke observed.

"Too bad she's not more lucid."

"She told a story the best way she knows how – in a blues verse," observed Hawke as he unlocked the car doors. "*Old* Suitman owned the Open Door and he shot someone." He turned the ignition and said, "Ergo, Stanton Senior shot a man."

She faced him with a mocking grin, "Ah, ye of the male species, who sometimes misses important subtleties. That can only be part of the story. Why would Stanton Junior be so reckless and determined to find a book if this mystery is simply about a murder which he didn't commit?"

"Billy devised enough red herrings to make a person dizzy from misdirection, but I've got his scent." Echo swung the pendant on the beaded chain. "We know this is a key which fits into an intricate filigree keyhole. We're looking for the other keyhole."

Hawke steered the car away from the curb. "And have you flashed on where we should look?"

"No. We begin again."

♪♪

Back at the Museum Store when Echo pressed Archer, he denied having any other small items that belonged to his great uncle.

He shook his head side to side rocking his dreads. "I'm telling you, Echo, I don't have any boxes like Mabel's or anything more like that trumpet case. All I have is a kitchen table and chairs that he built. Beautiful, unusual design. Probably go for a pretty penny now if I wanted to sell it."

Her intuition intensified, she couldn't contain her

exuberance. "Archer, please can we see them?"

Obvious that he doubted it would help, he agreed anyway. "Sure. I can't leave the store right now, but you're welcome to take a look. My apartment's a couple of blocks away." He fished the key out of his jean pocket and gave them directions."

Archer lived in a contemporary studio apartment located on the top floor of a converted industrial building. Blonde wood floors and pale walls contrasted with the dark brick wall, giving the illusion of more space. The Navajo blanket on the bed lent some flair to the interior, however the real artistic centerpiece sat in the space designated for the kitchen. Echo moved across the room to the four fleur de lis backed chairs surrounding a porcelain topped table.

"This set is a replica of the table and chairs Billy made for Mabel, except this one is a mahogany wood and the porcelain top is red."

"Do you think there is any significance to the fleur de lis design?" asked Hawke.

She stooped, running her hands under the table ledge. "I think everything Billy did, related to this mystery, has meaning."

Repositioning herself in a squat, she shuffled on the balls of her feet, inspecting inside and outside of the table skirts. "And here it is." She pointed to a filigree keyhole.

37

ROYAL STREET: *a mule and a carrot*

The faint peal of church bells from St. Louis Cathedral announced the two o'clock hour when they exited Archer's apartment building.

Hawke's phone rang at the corner of Royal Street. He said to Echo, "You go ahead to return the keys to Archer. I'll see what Moses wants, then drive the car around to the front of his store."

He spoke into the phone. "Hey, man. Everything go ok?"

His face darkened, troubled by Moses' warning about Nash. He disconnected and turned at the sound of a rumbling muffler. A white helmet hid the face of the man a block and a half away revving his motorcycle in idle. Hawke shouted, "Victoria, get off the street."

Echo looked back confused when Hawke called.

He waved his arms at the motorcycle. "It's Nash. He's furious about losing Zetta. Moses says he fired his gun."

The mule drawn carriage clipped by at the same

moment Nash released the kickstand with his boot. Echo jogged alongside the buggy, grabbed hold of a seat riser, planted one foot on the step plate and launched herself onto the floor of the carriage. The buggy bounced on its springs.

Jerome looked back surprised to see Echo pulling herself up from the floorboard. He started to rein his mule. "What the hell? Are you crazy?"

"Keep driving," she ordered pointing behind them. "Don't stop!"

Hawke jumped into the car and pulled into the light traffic behind Nash. He followed Nash, weaving the mini car in and around traffic as easily as the motorbike.

Echo knelt on the seat looking back, her hair falling loose after losing her clip.

Nash pulled up near the rear of the carriage. "Give me the book," he yelled.

She shook her head negative and shouted back, "I couldn't find it."

He throttled up his speed, cut around the back edge of the carriage, pulled up on the left side and reached into his jacket. "I'm not playing, witch!"

Frantically searching for something to defend herself with, Echo reached over the high bench seat and grabbed Jerome's whip with the dangling carrot. She waved the carrot in front of Nash's helmet. He swerved to avoid the distraction, removing his hand from his jacket to control his bike with both hands.

Nash revved the cycle's engine. Mr. Butler's gait changed to a trot. Nash increased his speed. The mule cantered. Nash speeded up. The mule broke into a gallop. Jerome struggled to control the mule's dangerous race through traffic.

At the sound of sirens nearby, Nash reached into his jacket again. Steadying his bike, he extended his arm, waving a gun at the carriage.

Hawke accelerated, nudging the back wheel of the motorbike with the front fender of the little green car. The bike wobbled. When Nash brought his gun hand back to the handlebar and managed to steady the bike, Hawke prodded the bike again. Nash lost control, laying the bike sideways on the tarmac. The bike skid another fifty feet up the street until it hit a trash dumpster parked by a construction crew. Nash jumped up from where he landed on the sidewalk and ran with a hop – he cradled his arm, his whole body leaning to the left. Leaving Nash for the police, Hawke followed the runaway carriage careful not to spook the mule further.

Curls falling around her face, Echo held tight to the seat back from her stance behind Jerome. "Can't you stop him?"

"I'm trying. He only wears a hackamore, no bit." Jerome pulled hard on the reins, calling to the mule, "Slow, Mr. Butler, Slow, man!"

Echo searched for some way to help. Maybe the carrot would distract the mule. She stretched over Jerome's shoulder holding the whip so that the carrot tapped against the mule's forehead and nose. Confused by the absence of a revving motor, the mule shifted into a disjointed gait, ducked his head and shook the bridle as if to throw off the braided rawhide bosal around his nose. Echo tapped his nose again with the carrot. Mr. Butler's abrupt stop jostled the carriage, the rigid wheels jerked and skewed sideways before the carriage settled on its springs at a ninety degree angle to the mule. Echo landed on the floorboard sliding forward under Jerome's feet. She held tight to the metal seat bars until the carriage resettled.

Sprawled between Jerome and the rear of his mule, Mr. Butler's tail switched over her face. Tangled curls splayed across her fair face concealing her eyes.

"Now this is a picture for our family album," Hawke drawled. His strong hands assisted Echo up into a sitting position. In a familiar display of tender humor, "Sweetheart, you bring new meaning to togetherness."

"And I love you, too." Echo brushed away the tangles and asked. "Where's Nash?"

"Last I saw, he was trying to run," pointing down the side street.

When Echo moved in that direction, he held her arm. His dark eyes flashed a gentle but firm warning. "Whoa, Warrior Princess. Let the police pick him up."

38

FRENCH QUARTER: *worst that could happen?*

Satisfied he had garnered all the information he could, the detective tapped his pen with the chewed tip on the yellow pad. "You can leave. We're done."

He followed Echo's eyes to the group huddled around a policewoman in the District station. Zetta's shoeless feet curled up under her on the hard straight chair, she gestured often to accent her story. Poppy borrowed a chair from another desk wheeling it close to Zetta. He toed his chair back and forth in a rocking rhythm while Moses looked down from where he sat on the edge of the detective's desk in a posture of power.

"They'll be here a while longer. Pretty outlandish story they have to tell. Not that your accusations aren't just as wild. If today was April first, I'd think you were fooling with me."

"Detective, trust me. There's someone who inspires more fear than you if I botch this."

Echo shivered at the nagging consequences of her transgression - acting in disregard for the unwritten laws and rules of the elite. Grandmother Esme would never forgive her if Echo's accusation of Stanton turned out to be wrong.

What's the worst thing that could happen?

39

UPTOWN: *arrogance and morons*

"Officer, I'm sorry I can't help you. Mr. Nash didn't appear for work today." Stanton leaned his stout body back in his burgundy leather executive chair, rolled the hand-shaped cigar absently between his fingers and returned the stare of the detective from across his desk.

"And you have no idea where he is?" the detective asked, incredulous.

Stanton eyed the detective with a supercilious air. "I believe that is precisely what I said."

Offended by Stanton's lordly manner, the seasoned detective stood up from the modern Italian chair, which probably cost more than his annual pay. He placed both hands on Stanton's desk and leaned in for emphasis.

"Mr. Stanton, a number of people identified Larry Nash as the person responsible for two serious felonies, kidnapping and assault with a deadly weapon. His actions are linked to recently discovered items, one of which is inscribed with initials matching your family monogram. Do you have any knowledge of what Nash was involved in or why?"

His face florid, Stanton puffed his cheeks out in irritation, "I'm appalled at what you're implying. My family has long been recognized for its philanthropic and civic participation in this city. Is your superior aware of your attempt to involve me in these abominations you've accused Nash of?"

"Sir, my superior is aware that I will follow all leads and treat all persons involved with the same respect."

The detective paused in the doorway. "Until we resolve this, I must ask you to check with us before traveling out of the state. Thank you for your time."

♪♪

He snatched the disposable phone from his jacket pocket and called Nash. "Do not come back here. You can stay at my hunting cabin in LaSalle Parish. And don't leave there until I call you."

"I think I broke my arm, boss."

"You can find a rural clinic once you're far enough out of the city."

Stanton gritted his teeth and swallowed. His face was flushed red from raised blood pressure. Exploding now would reap no further benefit.

"Did you find anything useful?"

"The Creole PI said they found a note, no book. The witch also said she couldn't find no book. That's good news ain't it, Mr. S? The treasure is probably long gone by now."

He hung up on Nash's grating voice and dialed another number. What a grave mistake - hiring this idiot whose thought process was equivalent of a twelve year old's. He folded the cigar over his middle finger, breaking it in two, and crushed the premium tobacco in his fist.

"Yeah. Who is this?"

Indignant at how the Mafioso Candela answered his call, Stanton ignored the question. "I need someone to clean up the mess that moron Nash left behind. This time, send me a professional or your own pants legs will get muddied from the splash."

Candela didn't argue. "Tell me where."

40

Carrollton Street: *electric air*

Violet opened the door partway to their knock, her face strained.

"I'm sorry to intrude, Violet. Are you feeling unwell? You look a bit feverish."

Violet reached out to touch Echo but abruptly dropped her arm to her side. Her lips parted into a curved, stiff smile. "I'm fine. Come in." She backed away, but didn't open the door any further.

Echo slipped through the doorway, instantly aware that she walked into trouble. Too late to warn Hawke.

A muscled left arm wrapped across the front of Echo's shoulder and around the side of her neck. He yanked Echo back against him, motioning with his revolver when Hawke sidestepped. "Ah ah. Don't you try to play hero. If all of you just do what I say, nobody gets hurt. Ok, now we're going to find what you came here for."

Hawke stopped moving, holding his hands out at his sides to indicate he wasn't a threat. Violet trembled next to him, the scarf on her head disarranged by the over-muscled man jerking her around prior to their arrival. Hawke reached out and held her hand to comfort her.

The man's posture pressured Echo's head forward. She raised her left hand, holding onto his wrist near her throat. *FLASH. Frigid. Stone-hearted.* Ok, he lied about not hurting anyone.

Echo's narrowed eyes bored into Hawk - conveying what?

She scooted two tiny steps back to find the balance and rooted posture taught her by Ms. Shu. Hawke tensed when he noticed Echo's eyes glaze with introspection then fire with fierce determination. He trusted his wife's senses, but couldn't predict what would happen next. Readying himself, he dropped Violet's hand after a quick squeeze to reassure her.

"You're lying," Echo spat, shifting her weight to her left leg.

Overconfident in his steroid enhanced muscles, the thug jerked her neck, his elbow swinging forward. Echo raised her right foot and kicked back against his knee to dislodge his balance. At the same moment, she swept her right hand across the front of her body connecting with the man's forearm below his elbow. Using his own mass for momentum, she continued her movement in a circle swinging his body around until the hand with the gun pounded against the wall. She ducked her head and bit his arm hard.

"You crazy bitch," he yelled, loosening his hold on her neck.

Hawke lithely stepped over and kicked the back crook of the thug's knee, tumbling him face down to the floor, but the guy managed to keep a hold on his gun. Hawke stood on his wrist to pin the hand that still grasped the weapon to the floor. The goon bucked, throwing Hawke off balance, rose to his knees and leveled his pistol at Hawke's stomach.

CRASH! Shards of a lamp globe scattered near where

the goon slumped to the floor. Violet dropped the lamp base and fainted.

♪♪

An unusual intrusion in this neighborhood, the intermittent whoop and oscillating colors on the light bars atop the police vehicles blocked Carrollton Street traffic. Patrons in the coffee shop next door crowded around the outdoor tables, fascinated with the sideshow. The man dressed in a dark suit shook his finger to emphasize a point. He didn't appear to be winning his debate over jurisdiction with the taller, stocky detective dressed in rumpled twill pants and a short-sleeve pullover shirt. With his slender build, beard and glasses the man in the suit resembled an academic more than a law enforcement officer. Snatches of their heated discussion drifted across the fence.

"..ongoing investigation..:

"local kidnapping.."

"FBI..."

The rumpled detective shook his head in disagreement, stubborn in his response. "...after we're finished with him..."

The exotic redhead moved away from the porch railing and planted herself between the two men. Although she spoke in an animated fashion, the patrons couldn't distinguish what she said - her voice husky and low. The slender man gave a quick nod in agreement. When the detective shook his head an emphatic no, she stomped her sandaled foot, poked her finger into his chest and kept talking until he also agreed.

Later, among themselves, the spectators disagreed about whether the air around her hair sparked or glowed, but they concurred it was electric.

41

UPTOWN: *a bully without a victim*

The long, melodious chime of the doorbell played out before Echo heard the sound of heels clicking across a floor. The door opened, revealing a large boned woman. Glossy grey hair cut into a bob framed a face void of makeup.

"Yes?"

"My name is Victoria LaBauve. I'd like to see Theodore Stanton."

The woman hesitated, her eyes shifting to her left.

Echo followed her gaze to an open doorway off the foyer. She raised her voice. "He's not expecting me, but I think he'll want to talk to me anyway."

"Uhm." The grey haired woman hedged, unsure how to respond.

Stanton called out in a belligerent tone, "For God's sake, Catherine. Show her in."

This wasn't household help as she first surmised. This was Stanton's wife. Echo reassessed the woman dressed in a straight black skirt, white blouse and low heels. She lightly touched Mrs. Stanton's arm, apologizing for intruding. *A sense of sadness and isolation - no deception.* She must remember to introduce Catherine to Poppy's healing touch after this.

His fleshy body posed behind a massive dark walnut desk in the center of the study. Behind him, a wall of curtained windows overlooked the front lawn. Stanton flicked his fingers to dismiss his wife, as if shooing a cat. "That's all, dear. You can shut the door on your way out."

Pulling the door softly behind her, Mrs. Stanton left without acknowledging either of them further. Echo noticed she left a small crack between the door and frame.

He dropped any pretense of congeniality. "Aren't you the brave one?"

"I wanted to speak with you alone, but I'm not a fool. Look out your window. My husband is waiting outside for me."

He swiveled his chair and lifted an edge of curtain, confirming Hawke sat in a car parked at the curb.

"The two goons you sent failed, so please no more guns."

"I don't know what you're talking about."

"I believe you do, but enough obfuscation." She withdrew a brown moleskin notebook from her bag and dropped it onto his desk. "I think this is what you are feverishly searching for."

His eyes flitted from Echo, to the book, to the door, waiting – a black scowl on his face.

"It's no trick. That's the real thing from 1940. Your father documented his own larceny."

"If this is real and you're giving it to me as you say, you'll have no proof."

"I have enough information to induce a federal investigation into the legitimacy of your holdings."

He snarled, his face a mask of cold malignancy, "Little girl, you don't know who you're dealing with."

Echo thought back to the thirteen year old frizzy haired girl confronting her cruel classmates. "I studied the psychology of a bully, Mr. Stanton, and you're nothing but a big bully. Your need to dominate masks an underlying fear that you are not in control. You perceive and retaliate against imaginary threats."

"Imaginary? You naive child. I would have lost everything. Everything!" he screamed.

"Everything is not material goods. What about your family?"

"What family? That woman out there who has the social quotient of a robot or the daughter she gave me who is more interested in the color of her lipstick than the family business." He sneered, "You don't understand."

"You're right. I don't understand. Family is my everything."

He grabbed the notebook off the desk, hugging it to his breast. "I'm suffering for the iniquity of my father."

What a self absorbed, unpleasant person. "You'll be punished for your own sins, Mr. Stanton."

With a grim purpose in every line of his face, he said, "I don't think so Mrs. LaBauve. You are hardly a credible adversary against someone with my reputation and stature in the community." He stood, "Our business is concluded here. I'll let you see yourself out."

Echo heard the swish of a skirt and steps moving away from the study door in response to a pounding at the front door. Had Catherine listened in to their conversation?

Two men and a uniformed policeman pushed past Catherine into the study. Hawke followed behind them.

"Mr. Stanton, I'm Special Agent Clark with the FBI." He held up his badge for identification.

Startled, Stanton said, "You."

The agent smiled and moved further into the study. "I believe you met Detective Mitchel earlier today."

The detective motioned for the uniform to cuff Stanton. "You're under arrest for conspiracy to commit kidnapping. And when we're done with you, the federal government plans to charge you with racketeering, among other things."

"This is outrageous." Stanton sputtered, his face ruddy with indignation.

The detective ignored his bluster. "In addition, Mr. and Mrs. Stanton, this search warrant authorizes us to search your homes, automobiles and office."

Hands cuffed in front, Stanton turned to Catherine, his expression thunderous. "Don't you say anything! Call my lawyer."

Catherine exhaled a deep breath, squared her shoulders and said, "I'm afraid you'll have to call him yourself, *dear*."

As the officer led Stanton past her, Echo met his icy glaze without flinching. She said softly, "Bullies need victims to survive."

42

HOME: *the ultimate keyhole*

Gathered around boiled crabs, crawfish and veggies piled onto the table covered in newspaper, their conversation buzzed over the fun music of Kermit Ruffins in the background.

The slam of the screen door announced Zetta with refills- six bottle necks caught expertly between her knuckles. "Water for Echo and Poppy. Beer for the rest of us."

"Hey girl, you really know how to handle those."

"A talent I picked up in college. Could've carried eight." She sat in the empty chair next to Archer and tapped her bottle to get everyone's attention. "So Echo, we're ready for the rest of the story -as Paul Harvey would say."

Eager to share the mystery solution, Echo recounted what happened.

The keyhole in Archer's table was a dummy. Although the key fit into the hole, it didn't turn. Hawke and Echo were on their way to Violet's when Nash showed up.

After the police took custody of the thug, they tried the key in Violet's table. The key not only fit into the hole, but turned, springing open a hidden compartment in the table drawer where, finally, they found the book. The contents of the note book were sufficient to get a search warrant for Teddy Stanton's home and office where the police uncovered five other incriminating notebooks.

Hawke added, "There is no proof who murdered Scarmuzi, so this is pure speculation. The police think Scarmuzi may have taken the notebook and tried to blackmail Stanton. Stanton shot him but was scared off by Billy and Mabel before he could recover the book."

Poppy asked, "What was so important in the notebook that Stanton Junior risked everything?"

"The majority of the Stanton family wealth is based on six hundred acres of oil rich land which they hold the mineral rights to. Stanton Junior knew from the other notebooks that property was illegally transferred to Stanton Senior in the thirties by corrupt officials working together with the mafia boss, Lucky DioGuardi. He didn't want to lose everything he had, for the sins of his father."

"A toast," said Archer raising his bottle. "To the Foundation and new found friends. Another mystery solved."

They clinked their bottles in celebration.

Echo laughed, "There's still more to the story."

All waited in anticipation.

"The professor and his wife are FBI agents. They'd been investigating Stanton for a year when they recruited Silverman three months ago. Consulting with Silverman on a political campaign was a believable cover story which allowed them to get closer to Stanton.

EPILOGUE

BREAUX BRIDGE: *tempest from afar*

Five-thirty. The blue glow of the digital numbers on the alarm clock illuminated the bedroom enough for Echo to find her robe laid on a chair back. She pulled the short kimono over her t-shirt and boxers and wiggled her long slender fingers along her scalp from forehead to crown, combing out tangled curls. Except for the pat of her bare feet on the wooden floors as she moved through the dark cottage, silence enveloped her.

Enticed by the aroma of dark roasted coffee, she shuffled into the kitchen. Empty. An empty mug sat on the counter - evidence that Hawke had been awake for a while. She loved the smell of coffee and had tried converting, but she still preferred ingesting her caffeine ration from tea.

Blotchy shadows danced on the walls in the muted light of the early morning. The recessed lighting had been dimmed, shedding only enough light to move around the room without banging into something. Echo selected Poppy's balancing energy blend from the assortment of teas in their pantry. Waiting for the tea to steep, she fondly remembered childhood moments spent with Poppy in the cottage's combination kitchen and dining space. She and Hawke had not changed much in the cottage. They had repainted the walls the same persimmon color that had brightened the room throughout her childhood.

A polished driftwood piece drew her attention. Hawke had hung the *Sunset, Sunrise* photographs. Removed from the fancy double frame used to display them at the gallery showing, they were now attached separately to the remains of a tree mounted on the kitchen wall. Hawke had selected and polished a cypress knee large enough to accommodate more photographs.

A frog, croaking in symphony with the insect drone and morning song of birds, called her to the screen door. The sweet, fresh scent of citrus blossoms hanging on the thick, moist summer air tickled her nose. A deep porch wrapped the small golden yellow cottage with burnt red shutters. In the days of working plantations, painted exteriors distinguished the French speaking inhabitants from the English speaking Americans who lived in white houses. From the porch, which overlooked an orange grove on the south side of the house and the Bayou Teche on the west, Echo scanned the oak trees standing sentinel from the cottage to the banks of the muddy water. Massive knotted limbs curved down resting their weight on the ground before stretching up again in gnarled splendor toward the sun.

She spotted a shoulder resting against a giant oak. His bare feet stood on the knobby roots which had erupted from the ground long ago. He had pulled on black jeans from the night before, zipping them but neglecting to button the waistband and foregoing his shirt. In the milky grey of dawn, a steam fog rose off the bayou in the background. On impulse she stole back into the kitchen to grab a camera Hawke kept on the shelf next to the cookbooks. She stood at the edge of the verandah, waiting and watching. Having heard the screen door open and close, Hawke turned his head back to the house in anticipation, his eyes as dark as the muddy bayou water. A lock of tousled hair partially covered his face... strong, yet yielding.

Click. Satisfied that she captured her Hawke at sunrise, she placed the camera on the verandah and walked across the damp grass to join him. She leaned back against his exposed chest, hugging his arms around her.

He rested his chin on the top of her head. "You're up early."

"Yeah, I'm dreading the morning, but I'm rested." She sighed then reminded him. "We escaped the city last night after celebrating without speaking to Grandmother."

"Yes, well," he laughed and summarized the news. "Headline - front page above the fold with a picture of you. *Socialite Closes FBI Case While Solving Mystery.* Someone captured you, hair flying wild when you waved that carrot on a whip to distract Nash."

"Well, I guess that about sums it up," she smiled.

Embraced against the sentry oak, Hawke and Echo kept their early morning vigil, attended by the peaceful lapping of the muddy bayou at its bank. The pale grey fog burned into a platinum steel air, quieting the insect drone.

The chirp of an incoming call on the telepresence screen drifted through the screen door. The system voice announced, "Esme calling."

ABOUT THE AUTHOR

Vickie Pettee grew up in the Heart of Acadiana where bayous and sugar cane fields were playgrounds, fireflies a summer evening delight and cousins your closest friends. She lived and worked internationally as a Global Vice President of Human Resources. After clocking more than two million international travel miles, she retired back in Louisiana, where she now lives with her husband, across the lake from bohemian New Orleans.

Socialize with Echo and her cohorts on Vickie's facebook author page.

♫

Vickie is at work on the next adventure in the Foundation Mystery Series. Her working title is Carousel *de*Frog.

www.ingramcontent.com/pod-product-compliance
Lightning Source LLC
Chambersburg PA
CBHW030917120626
46554CB00001B/181